WINGS OF DRAGCA

PROTECTED BY DRAGONS SERIES: BOOK FIVE

G. BAILEY

Cover design by Christian Bentulan.

Edited by Helayna Trask.

❀ Created with Vellum

Death or the throne? Queen or survivor?

Isola and her dragon guards are shaken after the events that forced them into hiding in Dragca Academy.

With the queen of the supernaturals on Earth offering Isola and what is left of her people a permanent home...will Isola leave Dragca to save the dragons she loves?

Or will the last dragon ice queen rise and kill her enemy, even if it means losing her heart?

Death has always been a curse on Dragca, and someone has to pay the price of fate...

18+ RH.

This book is dedicated to one of my closest friends who I met this year in Texas (though it seems like we have always been friends). She has helped me so much, in ways I didn't even know I needed help. I am certain I wouldn't be the author/person I am today without her love and guidance.
So, this book is for CJ.
I will always be thankful to have met you.

P.S. I'm also so, so thankful to The Cat's Pajamas for being in my life.

PROLOGUE

"*I* didn't expect to see you on your mating day, princess," Elias taunts as I get to the bottom step and see him resting on the side wall of the cage, crossing his arms. I run my eyes over his pale skin and dark eyes that match his black hair. This is now or never. I don't have time or a choice anymore. Eli must remember, even if what I'm going to do might kill us both.

"I had to do this. I'm tired of playing this cat and mouse game with you, Eli. You are mine, and you will remember me," I state, keeping my voice firm as I walk straight up to the cage. His eyes widen as I unlock the door, pulling it open and stepping inside. I leave the door open and chuck the key on the ground before standing right in front of Eli who watches me like the cat I know he is. Though he just doesn't know I am his equal in every way, and I will never run from him again.

"That was a bad move, naughty princess," he finally says and pushes up off the bars to walk closer to me. I stay very still as he places both his hands on my cheeks and moves his face inches away from mine.

"Nothing I do to save you is a bad move, Eli," I reply, gulping as his hands slide down my face and to my neck. I'm not shocked when he spins us around, pushing me against the bars as he tightens his hands on my neck. It's a half-assed attempt to kill me, because deep down, I know he doesn't want to. He knows it too, but he is so lost in the darkness, he can't tell me that. He keeps tightening his hands until I feel like I can't breathe anymore, but instead of panic, there is just acceptance that if he can kill me, he never truly loved me. I'd die to test what I am sure of.

His hands tighten further, and I grab his arms as my dragon roars in my mind, begging me to fight for my life, but I won't. Just as black spots enter my vision, tears fall down his cheeks, and I know I have to say something, do something before I pass out

and can't. I call my light in the way I have practised, and it blasts out of me in swirls that twirl
themselves around Eli. I see the light out of the
corners of my eyes, but I can't look away from him
as he lifts me off the ground, putting more pressure
on my neck.

"E-Eli...k-kill me if that is what you n-need to re-
remember."

CHAPTER 1

ISOLA

"*A*re you ever going to leave?" Elias asks, his face hidden in the shadows of the room, so I can't really see him as he speaks. His tone is unmistakeable though, so full of hate and disgust for me. It's been four days since I walked into this dungeon, not recognising the man I am in love with. Four days of him trying his best to get me to leave him alone…and none of it has worked, no matter how much it hurts.

The first day, he didn't stop screaming at me, throwing himself against the bars to try and attack me. Dagan, Thorne and Korbin tried to make me leave, but I know I can't. *Not yet.* It's easier to face

Elias down here than to go upstairs and pretend this isn't happening. I made myself a vow to save Elias, to make him remember us. I won't give up on that. The second and third day, he didn't speak a word as he sat against the wall at the back of the cage, hidden in darkness. I felt like silence was my punishment on those days. I almost missed his screams because it was a sign he was at least paying attention to me. The dripping of water, the distant sounds of people moving around upstairs, and Elias's cold gaze on me were all that existed then. Again, my dragons brought me food and tried to make me leave, but I stayed. I will never give up on any of my mates, and even though Elias is not mated to me yet, he is mine.

I almost jump when Elias speaks to me for the first time today. His voice is so familiar, so comforting even though the coldness in it is something Elias has never shown me until these last few days. Elias always used to be able to make me relax by simply being there. I hope the fact I'm staying here does the same for him. We soon figured out that Tatarina didn't only turn Eli against me, she spent her time convincing him that Dagan, Thorne and Korbin are the enemies too. That anyone who sides with the Dragice name is an enemy to the throne, to

Tatarina who he believes is his queen. Nothing they have said to him has made a difference in his opinion. Though he doesn't react when they speak to him, he loses it when I do. I know I am the key to his memory...I just don't know exactly how to jog it.

"Never. Not until you remember who I am," I eventually reply, crossing my arms in the cold room. Eli leans forward, an evil smirk on his lips.

"You are just a lost, forgotten princess who even her daddy didn't want around. You are no queen, you are barely even a dragon, Isola," he growls in anger, pulling at the collar on his neck.

"More hateful words, Eli?" I ask, crossing my arms. "When are you going to learn I love you so much that I won't ever give up no matter what you say?"

"When I kill you. That is when you will finally realise how much I hate you." His words are cruel, making my heart ache as he stands up and walks to the front of the cage. The darkness in his eyes seems to reflect off how pale his skin is. There are black lines crawling down his cheeks from his eyes now, and he looks so thin. The bruises haven't healed on his face and arms from the fight it took to get him here.

"Do you remember Tatarina killing you?" I ask him, the words feeling painful to even ask him, but I need to ask the difficult questions, or we will get nowhere. She killed my Eli, and I want to hear every detail because I need to know how much pain she deserves when I kill her. He grips the cage bars tightly, locking his eyes on mine as I stand up off the floor. My hands itch to rush to the cage, to hold him because my heart and body doesn't understand how Eli is different. My mind knows I can't do that and survive it.

"My queen would never do that to me," he replies, though his voice slightly wavers. "She told me all about you when I woke up from the magic you used to control me." I almost laugh at the crap Tatarina made up. Eli was never under any magic. He just loved me like I love him, even when curses and the entire world told us it was forbidden.

"Tatarina would think love is magic...and it is in a way, but it doesn't control you. I never controlled you, Eli. You are Elias Fire. No one could control you, and you chose me," I say, rubbing my heart when I feel a sharp pain. In this moment, I can relate to every woman in all the romance books I've read when a guy is breaking her heart. It feels like Eli is destroying me, but I know I can't give up on him. My Eli is hidden somewhere in the shell in front of me, I just need to find him. No matter what the price. It's never been easy for us.

"Lies!" he spits out. "You are nothing but a princess that wants a throne that isn't hers. Tatarina helped me, healed me, and I owe her my loyalty. When I get the chance, I will kill you to pay her back."

"I don't believe you," I say, walking up to the cage and keeping a good distance away so he can't reach me.

"Why don't you test it? Come in this cage with me, naughty princess," he taunts. My eyes widen at the nickname, the one he used to call me. I don't care that he is using it to call me to my death by his hand, I only care that he remembers it. He glares at me, scratching at his arms as I stand silent, watching him.

"That isn't happening. Ever," Thorne's cold voice echoes around the dungeon as I turn to see him stood at the bottom of the steps. I was so lost in my shock over Eli's nickname that I didn't hear him come in. My dragon didn't bother to warn me because she has been quiet since we got down here. Eli being like this hurts her too. She thinks of Eli as hers. "Isola, your people need to see you. You need food and decent clothing." I run my eyes over Thorne, his blond hair is brushed neatly to the side, he looks healthy and handsome. His new dragon uniform fits him like a glove, and his long dark blue cloak clipped around his neck with a Dragice crest pin makes him seem almost royal. His clear blue eyes meet mine just before he speaks privately into my mind so Elias cannot hear.

There is nothing we can do for him right now. Dagan is searching the library for answers, and your uncle is planning the war with Essna. It's important you come and join the meetings. There is news. Come with me and let me help you.

"I can't leave him, and I trust Essna to run meetings without me. I know nothing of war anyway," I say out loud. I know Thorne is right about me leaving the room, not so much about me attending meetings, though I'm scared if I walk away from Elias, he might try to escape or something.

"Elias isn't going anywhere, I will make sure of that," Korbin says like he can hear my thoughts and walks around Thorne who briefly nods at him.

Korbin looks different in the little time I've been down in this dungeon. His hair is shaved at the sides, the top part spiked up, and he has a dragon guard uniform on that is black with my family crest in the middle of it. Korbin comes up to me, placing his hands on my shoulders over my cloak. "Go and freshen up. Elias will remember, but until then, there is war going on outside of here, and you are the queen. They can't see you broken."

I sigh, knowing he is right. There is no point to any of this if we don't win the war, and I can't win anything if I am lost down here. I need to breathe and be with my other dragons. I can lean on them for only a moment before lifting my head again.

"Okay," I whisper, leaning up and gently kissing him, hearing Elias's long growl from right behind me. I turn to see smoke coming off his hands, and the collar is burning his neck as he tries to use his powers. I know jealousy when I see it. My Eli is in there somewhere, fighting to get back to me.

"Tatarina was right about you sharing your bed with more than one dragon. Why would I have ever been in love with someone like you?" Elias growls, harshly shaking the bars of the cage before giving up to walk back into the shadows of the cage. I know this isn't my Elias, but his words still burn a hole in my heart that I don't know how to recover from. Korbin kisses my forehead, whispering words of love before I walk to Thorne's side, letting him hold me close as we walk out of here.

CHAPTER 2

ISOLA

"My old room...it looks almost untouched since I left here," I say as Thorne opens the door, and I walk in first. Someone has made the bed up, lit three fire lanterns around the room, and placed a plate of mixed food on the end of the bed which has fresh white sheets on it. Bee's tree is gone, making me a little sad because I miss her, and two of the windows are boxed up with cardboard. There's one window not covered, and I look out to see three dragons flying past, patrolling the academy. The sight of them makes me feel a little safer. I'm sure my uncle and Essna have the place under strict control and monitoring while we wait for Tatarina's attack. The room smells slightly of chicken from the sandwiches and slightly of lavender from a plant someone has put on the bedside table. Surprisingly, my dragon grumbles in my mind, her eyes locked on the food I know she likes the smell of.

"I spent yesterday fixing it up as best I could. I had to take Bee's tree outside as it had rotted, but everything else was saveable," he tells me as he shuts the door. I turn and wrap my arms around his shoulders, pressing my body into his for the comfort I know Thorne can give me. He knows what it is like to be broken, to love someone who hates them. We were like that once, and we got past it because I knew the depth of my hatred matched the depth of my love for him.

"Thank you. I needed a bit of home, a bit of something to make this all seem better, and this is perfect," I explain to him.

I would do anything for you, Issy. Thorne gently whispers in my mind, and my dragon lets out a light purring noise in my head. She has been quiet the last few days, and the tiny amount of emotion I have gotten from her has been nothing but pain over Eli and indecision over what is best for the throne. Everything I am feeling too.

"Now, eat while I run you a nice bath. Can you do that for me?" Thorne asks, sliding his hand onto my cheek as I smile at him.

"Yeah, I am pretty hungry, now that you mention it...wait, do I smell that bad too?" I ask, and he laughs.

"No," he says, but I know him well enough to see through that little white lie. I guess I must smell as I've been in a dungeon for four days, only leaving for moments to use a bathroom and go back. I'm still wearing the same shirt and cloak I had on four days ago. I've been just existing the last four days, not aware of anything but what Eli was doing.

"You're lying," I reply, laughing when he winks at me before walking off to the bathroom. I walk over and sit on the bed, practically inhaling all the food as quickly as I can. I am starving because I refused to eat if Elias wouldn't. The thought makes me pause with a sandwich in my hand and put it back down. I could lose him, and nothing has changed while I was down there with him, at all. He is still stubborn and unrelenting in believing a word I tell him. I used to love that stubbornness about him, whereas now it is nothing but a pain in the ass.

"The bath is ready," Thorne says, coming out of the bathroom a few moments later. I put the rest of the food down and slowly drink some of the water before getting up.

"Thank you," I say, stroking his arm as I walk past him to the bathroom, leaving the door slightly open. I turn before stepping in, looking over to see Thorne picking up the tray off the bed. "You won't go anywhere, will you?"

"Never, Issy. I am just going to put this on the dresser and wait here for you," he tells me, and I feel his worry from our bond. I sense Dagan's worry as well which, mixed with my own, is difficult. I doubt any of us will be feeling much more than that emotion until this war is over.

"Thanks," I mutter, not liking how vulnerable I am at the moment, but I'm glad it's Thorne that sees it rather than someone I don't trust. I don't know when I started needing to have my mates around me, but everything with Elias and the war is making me want to hold them close.

Save our mates... my dragon hisses in my mind before leaving once again, leaving me stood in the middle of the room with a tear streaming down my cheek. I close the bathroom door before Thorne can see the tear and I look over at the deep bath which has sprinkles of rose petals in the water. Smelling a sweet scent in the air from the steam rising off the bath, I wipe the tear away and sigh. After pulling off my cloak, I fold it and leave it on the sink. I pull the shirt and knickers I'm wearing off, piling them next to the cloak before getting into the bath. The dirt and blood on my skin are difficult to scrub off, but I manage before finally washing my hair. After I'm clean, I get out the bath and dry off before brushing my hair which falls to the middle of my chest now. It's so long now, and I think I like it this way. I keep one towel wrapped around me as I leave the bathroom, leaning on the door as I look at my mate on the bed. He is lying down, reading a book, and doesn't notice me for a moment. When he does, his eyes widen, and he puts the book down.

"Th-There are clothes in the dresser for you," he says, clearing his throat, but a wave of pure lust and desire comes through our bond, making my knees weak from the sensation. I shake my head so I don't actually fall over before very slowly dropping the towel on the floor, with my eyes locked on his.

Thorne can't keep the lust out of his eyes, even as he opens his lips to protest before I slowly walk over to him as I place one finger against my lips. Thorne keeps still as I crawl on the bed and flip my leg over his hips, feeling how hard he is beneath me. His hands slide from the top of my shoulders down my back, sending shivers through me before he holds my hips. "You should be resting, Issy."

"I know what I should and shouldn't be doing, mate. I need to be close to you, to forget everything but you and me for a while. Can you help me with that, Thorne?" I ask, and he grins, moving his hands around my hips to my front. His one hand slides up my flat stomach to my breast, where he slowly rolls my nipple between his fingers as his eyes run all over my body. I moan, my back arching as I throw my head back, my hips bucking against him. Thorne's other hand finds my core, rubbing my clit in slow circles as he inches a finger inside of me. I cry out in pleasure, digging my nails into his chest as I come around his hand only a few moments later. Thorne flips us over on the bed, kneeling in-between my legs as he pulls his shirt off. I watch in fascination as he undoes his trousers, pushing them down to reveal his hard, long length. I don't have to wait a moment longer as he climbs on top of me, thrusting deep inside as I wrap my legs around his waist.

"Oh god," I whimper, just before he captures my lips, thrusting his tongue into my mouth and making me forget anything but the incredible feel of Thorne inside of me.

I love you, Thorne whispers into my mind as he thrusts in and out of me, his lips locked onto my own in a fevered passion.

I love you more, I whisper back, letting out a low scream as I feel Thorne come inside me, setting off my second orgasm. My head fell back into my pillow a few moments later, the world feeling like it's spinning in the best way possible. Thorne gently kisses me once more before rolling onto his back at my side. He wraps an arm around my shoulders, pulling me to lie on his chest as I link our legs together.

"I never thought I'd be as lucky as to have this with you," Thorne admits to me as I look up at him. He stares down at me with such love and understanding in his gaze.

"Neither did I. I'm happy we found each other, no matter anything else that happened. I wouldn't change a single thing because I'd never have fallen in love with you otherwise," I tell him, and he pulls a blanket over us, kissing my forehead. We lie together for a while, lost in the gift of being together before we have to face the sacrifice outside those doors.

CHAPTER 3

ISOLA

"You look amazing," Thorne comments as I finish braiding my hair in the mirror and tying the end with a hairband. It falls over my left shoulder, hanging on top of my light blue cloak that Thorne found for me. I've chosen to wear a dragon leather top and leggings, which are black with the Dragice crest embroidered above my right breast. Apparently, all these clothes were just left on the ruined staircase when they came inside of the academy. I don't know where Bee is, but this is a sign she is still on my side at least. Unless there is a hoard of light spirits we don't know about that are on our side, though I doubt it. This is a sign that she hasn't left me like I secretly fear she has. I can sense her in my heart, but I know she isn't near. I don't understand why she would have just left though. I shake my head, knowing I need to focus on anything else beside the thought of my spirit leaving me alone in the middle of a war that could easily take my life.

I stare at myself in the mirror as I lift my head, and for a brief second, I remind myself of a painting of my mother when she was younger—minus a crown. We have the same high cheek bones, bright blue eyes, and pale hair. Before, I always thought I never had the regal presence she did, but something has changed. Even without a crown, I think I am looking more like a queen every day. It's just because so much has happened that has forced me to grow up and face the consequences.

"What are you thinking about?" Thorne asks, smoothing a hand down my back as he steps to my side. I glance in the mirror at his eyes, the small tilt to his lips, and the content feeling drifting through our bond.

"About my mother," I honestly say, regretting it when Thorne's face drops into one of sadness. I feel the same emotion, only deeper, more painful than any look coming from him through our bond. "What happened when you faced her?" I say. I know he must have spent time alone with his mother, and nothing changed her mind anyway. I hate how much that must have hurt him and that I couldn't be there back then.

"My mother directed Elias to kill me, and that says it all. I thought I could be enough for her. That my mother would choose me over the darkness, but she couldn't, she wouldn't. There was a tiny moment when I thought..." he drifts off, lowering his gaze from mine in what I suspect is slight embarrassment that his mother didn't choose him. She should have.

"Thorne, she made the wrong choice. I don't understand how she could choose a throne over you. I wouldn't. I would give up the entire world of Dragca if you asked it of me," I tell him, and he lifts his eyes to meet mine once again in the mirror.

"I know, I would do the same for you. I have done the same," he gently reminds me, keeping his eyes locked with mine. "But I will never ask you to choose me. I only want your love, my mate."

"You never need to ask for that. It's yours. Even when I pretended I hated you, I loved you," I whisper just as he leans down to kiss me. The moment his lips touch mine, someone knocks on the door a few times. I sigh as he pulls away with a big smile before he walks over to the door, pulling it open. Thorne steps aside as Dagan walks in, flashing me a tired smile as he comes right up to me. Dagan looks exhausted; large dark bags are under his eyes, and his hair looks like he has run his hand through it a million times in frustration. I don't bother asking him if he found any news on how to save Eli in the library as he picks me up in his arms, holding me tightly to him as he briefly kisses me. I know the answer.

"Are you okay?" Dagan asks as he puts me down, and Thorne shuts the door. Dagan keeps his hands on my waist, our bodies close together. "I'm glad you have some colour in your cheeks and look so refreshed." His words make me feel guilty, like leaving Eli for only a little peace is betraying his brother.

"I haven't given up on Eli, you know that, right?" I start off but stop talking as Dagan kisses me again.

"I know you haven't, don't look and feel like that. Sense my emotions through our mating bond, you will see that I'm happy Thorne got you out of there for a bit. You do need to go and see your uncle before you go back to Eli," Dagan tells me, and I give him a shaky nod as I sense he is telling me the truth from his emotions. I place my hand on his cheek before gently kissing him.

"I will if you promise to get into bed and sleep for a bit?" I lightly ask, and he goes to argue no doubt as I carry on speaking before he has the chance. "And I will bring you food back. I'm not going to accept no as an answer."

"I can find guards I trust to watch Eli for tonight. We all need some time away from him to collect our thoughts. Kor should come up here with you if he doesn't have guard duty. It would be good for him to rest as he hasn't much recently," Thorne suggests, and Dagan nods in agreement with the plan.

"I'm not tired, but alright," Dagan replies, but I know he is lying from how tired he looks. "I could do with a bath before I sleep anyway."

"Yep, you definitely could," I say, and he grins at my teasing, tickling me as I escape his arms to run to Thorne who is laughing at us.

"Get out of here. Good luck with your uncle, and don't let the old fool boss you about. Remember who you are, Isola," Dagan firmly tells me.

"I know who I am now. You've all helped me realise it. I'm soon to be the queen, and I will speak to my uncle. I will not let him try to control me. Don't worry, and get some rest," I say determinedly, and he bows his head with a big grin. I chuckle and walk around Thorne to pull the door open and walk out. Thorne links our hands as we walk down the corridor, passing a few people carrying boxes and weapons who nearly trip when they see me, and they eventually bow.

"Where is everyone sleeping?" I ask once we've walked past them, their hushed whispers drifting to me. They are excited to see me. I don't really understand that because I'm still a princess, not yet crowned a queen.

You are the queen, my dragon huffs, like she can't understand why I would be confused why anyone is so excited to see me.

Yes, I know you believe that, I reply as she settles down.

"Thorne?" I question him again, noticing how he is watching my eyes, understanding that my dragon is speaking to me. I know there aren't that many rooms, and there must be quite a few people here now, much more than the academy is used to having, though I only have what little information Dagan briefly told me through our bond over the last few days. That Essna has half her seer army here, and the other half are people that cannot fight. There are new dragons coming in every day, survivors of Tatarina. Then adding those that we brought with us through from Earth, there are quite a few people in this academy now. I don't think it's enough to actually win this war, not with Tatarina's undead army, but no one needs to actually say that out loud right now. If I can find a way to save Elias, then I can kill Tatarina. Hopefully that means all her army dies with her. I need to kill her, so we can all have a future that is worth it. I squeeze Thorne's hand tighter as he answers my question.

"Most are using the old student and guard rooms, but the rest have opened up the old basement which is full of spare beds. There are long tunnels all under the forest which they are sleeping in and storing weapons in. The dining room stores food, and once a day, a team travels to Earth through the academy portal for more food and anything we need," he explains to me as we get to the top of the stairs, and I'm glad to know everything is getting organised, even slowly.

The stairs have been put back together with bits of wood and metal, and there is no dust anymore. I hadn't looked around until now since I hid my head in Thorne's chest on the way out of the dungeon earlier as I didn't want to see anyone. Dragons and seers are walking in and out of the main doors, which are now attached and left open. Most are dressed in weapons and cloaks, and there is so much light blue in the clothing. The colour of ice, even though a lot of the people here are fire dragons and seers, all hurt by the ice dragons who were meant to look after them. My father never looked after anyone but himself and his own interests.

There are tables set up, with people sharpening weapons on them and what looks like a lot of drag-onglass. At another table, they are making arrows with what looks like dragonglass tips that are hand-made. Everyone looks hard at work, getting ready for the war. It makes me feel a little guilty that I have been stuck in the dungeon all of this time. A few people notice me as I get to the bottom of the stairs, and they bow low. When they bow, it's like the whole room suddenly notices that I am here, and they stop one by one to bow as well. I watch it all in slow motion, and it's humbling to see. I gave up my chance for the throne for love and brought this war upon their shoulders, yet they still are bowing to me. Led by Thorne, I walk through the now silent crowd, around the staircase, and towards my uncle's old office.

It doesn't surprise me that it is the office he is reusing now, even if he isn't in charge of Dragca Academy anymore. I can't help but feel so angry at my uncle for his attitude towards me. How manipulating he came across, as I lift my head high while Thorne knocks on the door, and we hear my uncle shout for us to come in.

"Can you wait out here? I need to talk to him alone. It's about time my uncle and I have a long talk," I explain to him.

"Of course," Thorne says with a little, proud smile before he leans down and kisses my lips. I open the doors and walk into the office, shutting the doors behind me before facing my uncle.

"Hello, uncle. We need to talk."

CHAPTER 4

ISOLA

"I thought I would see you, *eventually*. Have you come to the right conclusion yet?" he asks, placing the book he was reading down and closing it. Every word is manipulative, making me feel guilty for my time wasted with Eli. I don't feel guilty though as I look at my uncle. I only see an angry, frustrated, old dragon who has lost all his family. Who has fought war after war, killing hundreds for the ice throne, the throne I walked away from and caused another war for him to fight in. I'm the last of his family, the last of the throne he fought so hard for, and he can't control me. I understand him, but I do not agree with his demands. I walk across the room to the window, looking out over the field and seeing the dragons and seers training. They are fighting each other, practising while Essna and another man walk around barking orders. Essna holds her head high, spinning a spear and her staff in her hands as she jumps, knocking a man straight across the field like he is a ball. It's almost amusing—the look all the men around her give her. They seem downright terrified. I move my eyes back to my uncle, knowing it's time we have a chat that may make him hate me. I don't want to lose any more of my family, but I will not be forced into he wants when I do not agree.

"What conclusion would *you* like that to be, uncle?" I reply, knowing his answer before he even speaks it as I eye his long red hair, tied back, and contrasting blue leather guard uniform.

"That one dragon guard boy is not worth the whole of Dragca falling into war and destruction! If that boy could remember who he was, he would tell you to kill him," he growls.

"If you had a choice between my mother and Dragca, who would you choose?" I ask him, glancing over to see his tense expression as he looks over at a painting on the wall. I follow his gaze, seeing it is a painting of two children. The one is my mother, and it wouldn't be surprising to find out the other is my uncle. I walk over, standing in front of it to read the small written message: *The Pendragons*. This painting wasn't here the last time I came into this office, I would have noticed it.

"I would have chosen Dragca," he announces, though I don't believe him.

"You would have been wrong *if* you did, uncle. Dragca might have fallen for another reason anyway. Especially without my mother on the throne," I reply. "The important thing is, you would have never been able to forgive yourself because you loved her. It would have haunted you, making you turn into a heartless monster that then could easily become a threat to the world you saved."

"It doesn't matter, your mother is gone, and Dragca is not long after her at this rate. I know I am right about the boy. He is lost, Isola. You have three other lovers, can you not let one go?" he angrily suggests, smoke rising from his hands where he is burning the desk.

"No!" I shout, slamming my hands on his desk, spreading ice across all of it and glaring at him as snow falls from the ceiling around us. "I am tired of you telling me what to do, uncle. I am not some silly child with no clue what she is doing. I am not your daughter. I am *not* yours to command. If all you plan to do is to second question my decisions, ignore my advice, then you might as well leave!" He looks shocked for a second as I keep eye contact, my dragon pushing to come out and fight my uncle to save Eli. There is a long, tense, angry moment before he smiles and leans back in his chair, crossing his arms. I frown, a little confused by his extreme change in emotions.

"Now, my queen, that is what I wanted to see. That is the fire that burned in the heart of your mother. That is the fire that should rule. I will not question you further, but only give my advice and guide you in what you think is right," he says, and my lips part in shock as I watch him, expecting him to change his mind and take it back. I expected anything other than what he actually said. The snow stops falling, but the bitter cold still fills the snow covered room from it.

"Are you suggesting you've been testing me this whole time?" I ask him, sliding into the chair near me.

"There is a good chance we all will die to save

Dragca. I want to make sure if there is even a slight chance you sit on this throne after this all, you will be a queen who is *never* questioned. That you will rule for a long time, have children who are respected and loved from their birth by all of Dragca. They will be loved because they are a part of the ice queen who saved Dragca and her strength made Dragca thrive," he explains to me.

"I want that also," I reply, sitting back in my seat. "Thank you for finally coming to my side without question." He bows his head, before crossing his arms.

"Now, what do you need of me?" he asks.

"I want to find a way to save Elias, so I can kill Tatarina. Do you have any clue how to do that?" I ask.

"I've been reading day and night to find an answer, but I don't have one yet. If you can jog his memory of how he was brought back to life, we may have a clue," he suggests.

"You've been researching?" I ask in utter shock. I look around at all the books on the desk, the ones piled on the floor, resting against the desk. All this time, he had been trying to help me when I judged him for it.

"I have nothing against the boy or your need to save him. I once had a wife and a child; when I lost them, I lost myself. I understand love. I understand the need to do *anything* to save them. I wish only happiness for you, Isola. If you love Elias Fire, then we will figure out how to save him," he tells me, deep sadness and regret in his eyes as he looks at me. I know it hurt him to even talk to me about this. He has lost so much.

"You had a wife? A-a child?" I stutter out, completely shocked. I never knew that, and it makes some sense as to why my uncle can be colder than my ice at times.

"They died, it's in the past, and I do not wish to relive those emotions. Even with family, Isola. I will say that your mother helped me through that time in my life, and now I will save her child because I couldn't save my own," his words are cold, yet so full of deep, dark emotions that it leaves the room in a deadly state.

"What was your child's name?" I ask, feeling the

need to understand him more and a strange feeling I must know.

"Emery," he says, his voice catching on her name.

"I'm so sorry for your loss. For your wife's death. I will remember my cousin's name until the day I die. I hope one day you will tell me more about them," I reply, knowing my words don't hold all that much comfort, but still I say them. He nods before rubbing his face and standing up. He walks around the desk and over to the middle of the room as I watch him, leaving footprints in the snow. He picks up the edge of the red rug and pulls it back, sending snow flying and folding the rug in half to reveal a little door. He pulls the latch to open the door and reaches inside, pulling out an old box by the handle on the top of it.

"This is how I escaped, back when everything went wrong and your father died," he tells me, shutting the door and pulling the rug back. "It leads to the forest, and it's safe, should you ever need to quickly escape."

"Good to know," I reply, watching him come over and sit on the chair next to me. He turns the chair to face me before putting the box on the floor between us.

"This was given to me by your mother. She gave me strict instructions to only give you it when you are the queen you are meant to be. I know that is who you are now, so it is time. I've never seen what is inside, but I knew my sister well enough to understand it was important," he says before standing up, no doubt to leave as I'm getting to understand my uncle now. I reach over and grab his arm before he steps away. "I am going to give you some time alone to open this."

"Don't. Stay, you are my family, and I need a family member here right now to open this," I ask him, staring into his hesitant eyes. "Please, uncle." He doesn't say yes when I plead with him, but he does slide back into his seat and waits for me. I look down at the old wooden box which has nothing but a crest I don't recognise engraved on the top of it. As I run my fingers over it, Louis explains.

"It's the Pendragon crest. When I die, so will it. Your mother always wanted your father to mix the Dragice and Pendragon crest together to make a new one for you. It just never happened," he tells me.

"It should have. It will one day. The two dragons could have the Dragice rose surrounding them and the swords behind. It will be a royal crest to be remembered," I whisper, though my voice sounds like a shout in the tense, silent room.

"It would be an honour to see a crest like that," he replies and straightens his back. "Now stop stalling and open the chest."

I nod, knowing he has read me like a book because I'm scared of whatever might be inside this chest from my mother. I'm scared how it might break my heart to open it. I take a deep breath before undoing the clasp and pulling the box open. I see the crown straight away, not believing my eyes as I look at how beautiful it is. It's not my mother's crown from the paintings or the one Tatarina stole, so I don't get whose it is. I lift it out of the box, looking at the detailed white and blue stones that are held between swirls of silver and gold. It's very striking for a crown, and I have trouble looking away from it to my uncle, wondering if he knows what it is.

"I can't quite believe my eyes," he mutters, reaching over to gently touch the crown. I look down in the box, seeing a letter at the bottom of the box.

"Here, you can hold it. There is a letter," I say, and my uncle happily takes the crown, holding it in the light as he looks at it in greater detail, though his eyes stray to the letter, and I know he wants to read what his sister has said. I pick the letter up, running my finger over my name that is written on the outside. I open up the letter and take a deep breath before reading it out loud.

To my sweet baby Isola,

When you read this, you will no longer be a baby but a woman—no, much more than that, a queen of Dragca. I write this as you lie in the cot near my bed, happily sleeping after a feed, and it breaks my heart to know you will be in danger.
A danger that is impossible for me to even imagine, but I will do everything in my power to protect you.
My Isola, you are the balance that has been waited for. A dragon is prophesied to hold both light and dark magic. You must bond with both the spirits, or the price will be Dragca's fall. I know there is much pain for you to overcome to reach this ending, and that I cannot save you from that pain. I

know that my life is short, and I will not see you grow up. I wish I could be there on your mating day, but in my mind, I envision how beautiful you will look. How happy. I wish I could be there to see the woman you will become, because I know how amazing she will be. I am so proud of you, no matter the choices you make.

I can leave you a gift, one given to me, but I never wore it as I knew who it should be worn by. It is the crown of the first ice queen. She was the daughter of Icahn Dragice, and she hid this crown when she died, along with her father's legendary spear. This crown is for you to wear as you face the final battle. I know the spear will be gifted to you by the same fate who gave me the crown.

I can only wish you a life of love and happiness. A life I never had until the day you were born, my sweet girl. Hold your head high. Be kind. Be loved and love back in equal measure. Please don't cry for me.

I will love you always, and we'll no doubt see each other in the stars one day,

Your mother,

Queen of Dragca.

I turn the note over, breaking down into tears as I see the crest drawn in the corner of the letter. The perfect mix of Pendragon and Dragice. Just like what I said before, and I know it is my crest she wanted me to wear. I feel like my mother is really gone now, this letter is so final. To my surprise, my uncle comes to me and embraces me, holding me tightly to his chest as I cry. It's a long time before I can pull away and take a deep breath as I wipe my face. The crown rests on the desk, and I stare at it for a moment in silence.

"Can you have someone make my new crest? I want to change my royal name as well. To reflect who I am. I am not my father's daughter. I am my mother's. Her real name was Merida Pendragon. My name is Isola Pendragon. Like it should have always been," I tell my uncle. He nods, a tear streaming down his cheek as he accepts the note from me, rubbing his thumb across the crest drawing. I won't hold the Dragice name on the throne any longer. My father was nothing but a cruel king no one should be proud of. I stand up, reaching over to pick the crown up before walking to the window. I watch myself in the reflection as I place my new crown on my head, declaring myself the queen I am going to fight to be. I look like the queen I was born to be. Isola Pendragon.

CHAPTER 5

ISOLA

I pull the doors open to see Thorne laughing at something Korbin said, and they both turn to look at me with wide eyes. The crown seems to have shocked my mates into some kind of silence. Even though Korbin and I aren't mated yet, at this rate, I'd be surprised if he still loves me enough to make the leap. We really haven't had much time together in ages, and I have mated to Dagan and Thorne in that time. I haven't even asked if he was okay with that. We seem to just be pulled apart right now, and it scares me more than I want to admit. I know he loves me though, I can see it. I love him too, and I hope that is enough.

G. BAILEY

"Hey, are you guys alright?" I ask.

"Wow, you look like a true queen," Thorne whispers, reaching out and lovingly touching my arm.

"Thorne, could I have a word?" my uncle says from behind me, and I turn to let him see Thorne. Thorne looks towards Korbin who nods in some agreement.

"I will be with Isola, and three guards are watching Elias while Dagan sleeps, go on," he says, and Thorne walks past me, gently squeezing my hand as he passes, then shuts the door behind me as I step closer to Korbin.

"It's been a while since we've been alone," I blurt out, and he steps closer to me, placing his hands on my upper arms as I stare up at his dark green eyes.

"I know, doll. I've missed you more than you could possibly know," he tells me before leaning down, kissing me sweetly. I sigh, wrapping my arms around his neck as he grabs my waist and deepens the kiss. It feels like coming home after a long trip when I'm in Korbin's arms. He is my home.

"Son, can we have a word?" Korbin's mother says, and we pause, gently pulling away in shock a little.

Korbin keeps his arm around my waist as we both turn to see his mother and father standing a short distance away. They have on long brown cloaks emblazoned with my father's crest, but they look okay after everything that happened before. Well, his mum doesn't look impressed, whereas his father has a big smile on his face. Korbin leads me up to his parents, stopping a little distance away.

"Princess Isola, how lovely to see you again," Kor's father says, offering me a hand to shake. I shake his hand as I reply.

"I am queen now," I inform them both, and his eyes widen only a tad, "though it's good to see you both. I was worried after everything that happened with the seers and Tatarina."

"That dragon bitch cannot kill us that easily," Kor's mother replies, shocking me with her hate-filled words, and she very slowly runs her eyes up and down me. "I know you gave up the chance to kill her for Elias Fire."

"Yes, I did," I reply, holding my head high because I will not apologise to anyone for the choice I made.

"Until I heard what you did, I did not want you with my son. I did not think his life would be more important to you than the throne. Now I know you chose love over anything else. Can we start over, as I truly believe you are what is best for my son and the whole of Dragca," she asks and offers me a hand to shake. I keep my eyes locked with hers as I shake her hand and nod my head once.

"I'd love that," I reply, and Korbin lets out a long sigh.

"Finally," he says, making us all laugh.

"Why don't we all go for a cup of tea? I've heard humans from Britain love tea," Kor's dad suggests. That is a good idea.

"They do, and luckily I was brought up there, so I know how amazing tea can be. A hot cup of tea fixes literally everything," I reply as we start walking, following Kor's parents.

"Then that's what we shall do. I even hid some chocolate biscuits," Kor's dad says, and I chuckle. We follow them past the stairs and to the left, which leads into the dining room. There are tables everywhere, far more than there used to be in this room, and everyone is covered in boxed food, weapons, blankets and everything you could need. I watch as every person we pass stops, staring at me in awe before bowing until I've walked past them. It's an effect I will have to get used to. I need to start believing I will be queen to all if I am going to make the rest of the world believe it.

We walk right to the back of the dining room where there is a row of kettles, clean cups, and containers with what looks like tea, coffee and even hot chocolate in them. We have to wait in a queue for the kettle before making our own drinks, and Kor's dad gets a new packet of chocolate biscuits out of a hidden box under the table. Kor's mum just rolls her eyes before we go outside the dining room to a room just behind it, which is again filled with tables but these are empty. We all sit down, and Kor's dad opens up the packet, putting it on the table in front of us. I dip a biscuit in my tea before eating it and sipping the tea slowly.

"I believe we should plan my son's and your mating ceremony this week," Kor's mum randomly states, and I choke on my tea. Literally. *Way to be cool, Isola.* Kor pats my back as I calm down and look at his mum with wide eyes. "I'm sorry. I didn't mean to take you by surprise, but I am sure you have thought about mating by now."

"Yes, we have discussed it, but a lot has happened since—"

"Have you changed your mind?" Kor interrupts, his voice full of pain as I turn, staring at him with wide eyes.

"No! I honestly thought you might have changed your mind," I admit, and I can visually see his relief as he puts his tea down and cups my face.

"I will never change my mind about you, doll. I'm completely in love with you, no matter what life throws at us, that won't change. I am yours, don't ever question that," he tells me, kissing me hard to emphasise his point before letting me go.

"Okay then," I say, quickly wiping a tear away and turning to Kor's parents, who look happy as they both smile at us. "I think a mating ceremony would be a good idea too."

"I'm happy you think so. The people need some happiness, something to remind them what they're fighting for. A royal mating ceremony would be the perfect way to uplift everyone's spirits."

"I agree," I say, leaning my head on Kor's shoulder as he links our hands under the table. Kor starts talking to his parents about something as I stare down into the dark water of my tea, the darkness only reminding me of Elias and how he won't be at the ceremony. I don't even know if we will ever get a chance to mate with each other, but I know I will fight forever to find a way.

CHAPTER 6

ISOLA

"*D*o you want to come in?" I ask Korbin as we get to my door after a long day of walking around the academy and seeing all the work that has been going on. I was amazed at how much has changed since I've been in the dungeon with Eli. They have kitted the entire academy out for the war everyone knows is coming. I just hope we survive it. I know Tatarina won't give us long. I'm going to spend my time with my dragons, getting Eli to remember, and with my people. My people were happy when they spoke to me, happy to fight for me despite the darkness we are surrounded in. My heart bangs as I think of Bee, knowing she is out there and still not back with me. I don't like it. "Are you going to sleep in here?"

"I'm on night guard until five in the morning, but I will join you then. Dagan has the night off, go rest with him. He misses you, and though he might not say it out loud, he can't cope with how Elias is right now," Kor informs me, and I nod, knowing that Dagan is taking Eli's condition as well as I am. *Which is not well at all.*

"I don't think any of us are coping well with how Elias is, but we have to just get through it," I reply, and he smiles, stepping closer so my back hits the door, and he pushes his body into mine. I kiss him first, making him chuckle low in his throat before he kisses me back. His hands slowly slide up my body, before guiding into my hair before he pulls back.

"I can't wait for our mating night!" he exclaims against my lips.

"Are you going to make me wait until then?" I ask in frustration, biting down on my lip as his dragon eyes burn red for a moment and then go back to normal.

"I'm going to tease you every chance I get until I can finally have you as my mate, doll," he tells me, sending shivers across my skin as he traces my lips with his own before stepping back and bowing his head slightly. "I will see you later, my queen." I chuckle at his unneeded formality before he turns and walks down the corridor.

Must save our mate... My dragon suddenly rouses to the surface as I place my hand on the door. I know she doesn't want me to go and see Dagan. She wants me to spend more time with Eli...and I can't tonight. I need a night away from him and the pain it causes me to be near him right now.

To save our mate, I need to be okay. Eli is hurting me right now. He is hurting Dagan. Dagan and I can fix each other. I am not giving up on Eli. I promise, I tell her, and she huffs in a mild agreement before sinking to the back of my mind once again. I breathe out the breath I was holding and slowly open the door, letting myself in. I shut it behind me and walk in to see Dagan sleeping on the bed, his arm cuddling my pillow as he sleeps. I smile before quietly taking my crown off, placing it on my desk, and stripping out of my clothes so I'm only wearing a vest and panties. I climb into bed next to Dagan, removing the pillow and letting him pull me against his chest. I breathe in his musky, smoky scent that instantly has me relaxing. I don't know how long I happily lie in his arms, listening to his heartbeat and breathing in his scent like he is my own drug. I never want to move in these moments. I would happily lie here forever.

"Waking up with you is always amazing," Dagan gravelly voice says, his breath moving my hair as I turn my head to look up at him.

"Even when I have morning breath? Like, that can't be nice," I say, smiling.

"Are you suggesting I need to brush my teeth?" he asks with a grumble, and I laugh.

"No, you smell like fire no matter what time of the day. You taste like fire too," I admit to him.

"Do I?" he chuckles, rolling us over so I'm lying on his chest, looking down at him. "You taste like magic. You taste like peaches but far sweeter and more seductive," he says, leaning down and kissing me like he is desperate to remind himself how I taste. I moan into his mouth, tasting nothing but the fire I spoke of and Dagan. He is addictive, making me want more with every stroke of his lips against mine. The passionate way Dagan rolls my hips against the hard length I can feel tells me he finds me just as addictive. I pull Dagan's shirt off, breaking the kiss for only a moment as he pulls it off. I go to tug my shirt off, and he catches my hand, placing it above my head. I gasp as he uses his shirt to tie my hands together.

"Keep them there for me, Issy. Oh, and trust me," he says, his words turning me on as I nod. I've never seen this side of Dagan, but damn, am I happy to play along. I gasp as Dagan rubs his hands over my breasts, covered only by my top, making me gasp. He chuckles at my reaction and winks before lifting his hands off my chest. He lights his hands up, and my eyes widen as he spreads pure fire all over my skin, burning away my top and panties as they go, making me gasp from the heat. The moment my panties are gone, Dagan is sliding a finger inside me as he twirls a tongue around my nipples. I moan, fighting the urge to move my hands as he drives me crazy. The mix of the danger of the fire and the sexy way Dagan is controlling my body edges me near an orgasm with every second that passes. Just as I get close, Dagan removes his hand and kneels up. I watch him slowly unbutton his trousers, using every second to tease me as he pushes them down, freeing his hard length. He strokes himself a few times as he watches me, teasing me further.

"You are such a tease, Dagan Fire. Are you going to

leave your queen waiting?" I ask. His eyes burn with fire for a moment before he grabs my hips, dragging me down the bed. I gasp as he suddenly flips me over, before pulling my hips up and sliding inside me in one fluid motion. I'm so sensitive that I can only grab the sheets, riding out the intense orgasm that instantly slams into me. Dagan thrusts in and out of me, riding my orgasm. I gasp as he suddenly pulls out of me, rolling me over and holding my hips as he guides himself back into me once again. He leans down and kisses me harshly, both of us breathless and chasing another orgasm.

I love you, my mate, he whispers into my mind, before leaning up and grabbing his shirt. He burns it away, replacing his shirt with his hands as he thrusts in and out of me.

I love you more, my mate. My Dagan, I reply and cry out as he finishes inside me, setting off another orgasm for me. I collapse to the bed as he lets go of my hands and holds me close to his side as we both get our breath back. When we've calmed down, Dagan pulls the blanket over us, and we face each other. I place my hand on his chest for a moment before he covers my hand with his and links our fingers.

"How was your day?" he asks me.

"Pillow talk, huh?" I tease, and he chuckles low as I answer, feeling my eyes drooping a little as I actually answer his question. "I spoke with my uncle, and the conversation ended with us hugging. Oh, and I changed my name to Isola Pendragon."

"Well, that sounds like you've had an interesting day. I think the name suits you," he says, and I love that he just accepts my choice without questioning me. He just knows it's something I needed to do, and he has accepted it. I know Dagan is always on my side. I smile as I drift off to sleep, not able to fight it any longer but knowing he will keep me safe no matter what.

"Morning, Eli," I say, walking into the dungeon, each little noise from my footsteps on the stone seem to echo around the dungeon. There are three lit fire lanterns in the room that were not in here yesterday, and they reveal most of Eli's cage now, so he cannot hide, I suspect. Eli sits silent, unmoving, and looking so close to death that it is hard to look at him. I have to mentally remind myself that my Eli is somewhere in him, just lost for now. It's my duty to find him. I get to the bottom of the stairs and nod at the two guards in here after they bow.

"Welcome back, my queen. We have given him

food, but he has not eaten it," the one guard with a deep voice explains.

"Thank you. You can leave us now," I reply, moving my eyes from the shocked expressions on their faces to my Eli.

"A-are you sure?" the other guard splutters out. "He is dangerous."

"Not to me," I confidently reply, stepping aside and waving a hand at the door at the top of the stairs. They quickly bow and walk out of the room, shutting the door at the top. I walk over to my usual spot by the wall and open my book, diving head first into the pages I love so much. It's not long before Elias gets up off the floor and comes to the front of the cage. He speaks just as the main the character in my book gets her first kiss. *Dammit.*

"What are you reading?" he asks, his voice a whisper that no doubt reflects how weak he is.

"It's a romance. There are two people who are soulmates, despite the entire world wanting them apart," I explain, knowing I picked this book up from the library because some part of me understands the love. It's very much like Eli and me. Torn apart by the entire world, but still fighting for each other because our souls know we belong together. Even if Eli can't remember that at the moment.

"Do they end up with each other?" he eventually asks, his eyes locked with mine.

"Yes. Sometimes love can be enough to survive anything," I reply, not being able to hide the emotion in my voice. I don't want to seem weak around him, but I also will not hide myself from Eli.

"I'm not who you think I am. I am not yours," he replies, though his voice cracks.

"What does your dragon say?" I ask, curious. Eli once told me his dragon has always thought of me as his. From the very first moment we saw each other across the corridor of this very academy. It feels like such a long time ago now, though.

"Nothing," he replies, and I frown at him.

"My dragon calls you mine because that is who you are to me," I tell him, and my heart seems like it's beating out my chest as he stares back at me for a moment. His eyes are so black now, so touched with a darkness that I can't see if he is speaking to his dragon or just looking at me. I can't sense much about him either, despite how much that hurts. I used to be able to understand Eli like I understood myself. The more time I spend down here, the more I doubt I can save him and get him back. The thought of that at all makes me want to break down.

"I am not yours!" he growls, making me jump as he shakes his head and falls to his knees, screaming out with pain. I drop my book and run over to him, desperately wanting to stop whatever is causing him pain. I try to reach through the cage to touch him, to see what is wrong, but he crawls away from me, shaking his head. "Leave. Please." His words are softly spoken, a despair-filled plea.

"If you promise to eat, I will go," I finally force myself to say, looking at all the trays of food in his cage. If I have to leave, I will make sure he is at least eating.

"Fine," he replies, to my shock as I didn't expect him to just agree with me. I stand up and walk out, doing what I promised I would do even if it hurts my heart with every step. The two guards are waiting outside, and they bow as I come out the doors.

"Can you watch him again? If he doesn't eat any meal, tell me. Alright?" I ask them.

"Of course, my queen," one of the guards says before they both bow once more. They quickly go back down into the dungeon, pulling the door shut behind them. I stare at the door for a moment, lost in my thoughts of how Elias talked to me just then. There was more of my Eli, but not enough to make me feel any better. I lean closer and rest my head against the cold stone, letting it take me away for a little bit as I focus on only it. I don't know if cold and confused is any less painful than angry and mean with Eli. Either way, every visit with him is hard to swallow and hard to forget. If he doesn't remember before Tatarina comes…well, I want a few moments with him before that fight which I might lose. I want to tell Eli I love him, tell him there isn't anything I wouldn't do for him, and have him be my Eli for a little bit.

"Queen Isola," Essna's voice snaps me out of my thoughts, and I turn to face her. She is dressed for war, with mostly leather clothes, dozens of weapons littered on her, and her staff with her glowing orb held in her one hand. The scar on her face always makes me want to question what exactly happened,

61

but I don't. It doesn't take away from her natural beauty anyway. I wonder if she ever puts the weapons down, as she always looks like this when I see her. I'm glad she is here, as we haven't had much chance to speak to one another recently. Her eyes drift from me to the door and back, before she nods her head to the side, suggesting I walk with her. I don't say a word, only lowering my arms and walking next to her as we leave the entrance to the dungeon, heading through my people to the outside. "How are you? Your dragon guards?" Essna's question takes me by surprise. I never had her down as one for small talk.

"There hasn't been much change. I feel like I will need to do something drastic to get him to remember me," I tell her, trying to keep my voice stronger than how I am feeling. "Dagan, Thorne and Korbin are just keeping themselves busy and trying to help me because they don't know what to do either."

"I believe waiting for your light spirit to return is your best course of action. She would not have left you if there weren't a reason," Essna says as we get to the main doors and walk out into the cold, crisp courtyard. The wind blows against my skin, the bitter cold to it feeling like a slap in the face almost. I pull my cloak around my shoulders as we walk down the steps.

Dragca Academy looks nothing like it used to, and yet I'm so thankful we are safe here for now. The trees look close to falling down, their bark rotting away and their leaves nothing but black shells of the lush green leaves they once were. Winter in Dragca does bring the death of trees, the loss of their leaves, and the fading of their colour, but there is always the promise of rebirth in the spring. Right now, there is no promise. Everything here feels lost in a darkness that will take more than just the trees around us, it will take the very heart of Dragca and destroy it.

"I would have liked if she told me this reason she had to leave first. I feel I am beyond clueless to what spirits are and their actions. I can only trust Bee has something in mind and it is worth me spending every hour worrying about her," I reply. Things are bad enough with Eli and the pressure of being queen to people I am going to lead into war soon; I can't lose Bee on top of that.

"Without a doubt she does have a good reason. You must trust her. I know Bee seems like your child, your responsibility, but light and dark spirits have been around for a very long time. They are full of wisdom we could never understand, and we must trust that Bee has a plan for us all," Essna says as we get to the grass and step onto it, hearing the dead grass crunch under our boots. "I want to test something. Would you give me some of your time?"

"Yes, but I want you to answer a question for me first," I reply, knowing well enough that I might as well try to ask something in return.

"Is it about the future or your dragon guards?" she asks me, her eyes curious. "As I could not tell you anything I have seen of them. It would be pointless anyway; the future is changing every time I look. The world—and its magic—is not in order."

"No, it is not about them. It is about someone else in the present," I ask her.

"Then ask away," she replies, nodding her head.

"How is my sister?" I ask her, and Essna pauses, closing her eyes as she touches the orb on top of her staff. I wait silently for a while, looking down at my own staff swirled around my arm. The red gem seems to glow here in Dragca. Essna finally looks at me, a tiny smile on her lips.

"Melody is alive and well. I cannot tell you more, though I am happy you asked me to look," she says, and I smile as she takes a deep sigh of relief. "Good news is coming swiftly." I don't take in her statement as I focus on the fact Melody is okay, and that means Hallie must be as well. As long as they stay on Earth, they will survive this all.

"I didn't know seers could find just anyone so quickly," I reply after a long silence between us.

"Melody doesn't know it, but her mother was my cousin. Melody is family to me, so are you in a very distant way. I do not need a lot of power to watch those who are related by blood," she explains to me.

"I didn't know that. I'm sorry I ever distrusted you," I reply. If I knew how connected she and Melody were, then maybe things would have been different for us all.

"You were right to distrust me, as much as I was right to distrust you when we met. The throne, the secrets of Dragca, and everything Dragca has become make anyone distrust a stranger. Only a stupid person would blindly trust anyone here," she replies to me, looking into her glowing orb for a moment before meeting my eyes.

"What was it you wanted in return?" I ask her because I want to go to the library, find a book and get lost in it for a little bit. I miss reading, I miss being me and grounding myself in the way that reading can do. Though I might avoid anything too dark with how I'm feeling. Essna smiles, bowing her head before sitting down on the grass. I stare at her strangely as she pats the ground for me to sit next to her. I do, stretching my fingers into the dead, yellow grass and looking up at the black trees in the distance. It feels wrong to touch the ground, and a deep part of me feels the sickness in my land. *One caused by Tatarina.*

"You are bonded to a light spirit, and a dark spirit did this. I wonder if you can heal the ground a little? If you practised every day, just as far as you can push it without Bee here, you could learn how to heal all of this. You could learn to use light magic on your dragon guard," she suggests, and I sharply look at her. I've never thought of using light magic on Eli. Maybe it could save him, maybe it could actually kill her if it destroys the bond he has with Tatarina. It would be a massive risk, one I don't want to do because I have to find another way to save him. But it can be a last resort…one I will only use if I believe Eli needs it.

"That might kill him," I finally reply to her, the cold breeze pushing my hair around my shoulders and making me shiver.

"Light magic is pure. It only heals, not destroys. It might be the only way you can truly save him," she replies to me. "I would very much like to see you try to use it, Isola. I will be here to stop you if anything goes wrong."

"I will attempt it," I reply, shrugging. "I can't see it doing any real harm."

"Good. Now when I use my power, I don't imagine it. I don't even picture what it can do, I just trust my heart to do what it needs. I trust my body, my soul to use my power hidden in the depths of it," Essna explains to me.

"It sounds like how I connect to my dragon. She and I are one. I can trust her instincts, well, most of the time," I reply, not mentioning how she is a little more kill happy than I am, and I have to calm that down a tad. Light magic isn't like my dragon though, it's different. More powerful than I can imagine. Essna nods.

"Now try connecting to the part of you that can access light magic. I am sure you can do this, Isola," she tells me. I give her a small nod before closing my eyes and feeling only the dead grass under me, the emptiness of it. There is no light here, nothing to pull on so I must find it within myself. I shut out all the sounds I can hear. I shut out the smell of dead, rotting plants and the distant scent of fire. I block out the comfort of my dragon in the back of my mind, as I know she cannot help me do this. I search for that part of me which is light, pure power. I know when I've found it because it feels like the sun is shining on every part of my body, making me feel so warm and comforted. I sense Bee a great distance away, and I know she senses me as well as I connect more to the power that binds us. The more I mentally reach for the light, the hotter I feel, the more my whole body seems to be on fire, though I suspect it is not. I gasp when the power suddenly goes, and I'm left shaking as I open my eyes. The sight in front of me is nothing like I expected to see. There is green, healthy grass, as tall as my knees, covering the ground and flowers growing everywhere around me. Dragca Academy looks more alive than I've ever seen it, and everyone has stopped to stare in awe as I look around. I can't see a dead tree, plant or even a little bit of brown grass for miles.

"Astounding," Essna gasps, standing up with me. I shake a little on my legs, and she reaches out, holding me up for a moment as I see everything surrounding the castle is now green. From the vines covered in white flowers climbing up the castle to the green, red and yellow trees, the grass, the flowers—it's all beautiful. Every dragon I can see suddenly falls to their knees, bowing their heads one by one. I can only stare around me, lost in this moment.

"I'm stronger than I thought," I quietly admit, and she bows her head with a large smile, her eyes drifting around at the beauty I struggle to take my eyes off of too.

"If you can save all this, then with practice, you must be able to save Elias Fire." Her words give me hope, something I didn't know I could have for Eli.

CHAPTER 8

ISOLA

"*A*re you ready yet?" Essna asks, knocking on the door as I look at myself in the mirror and take a deep breath because I damn well need it. I don't remember the last time I was so nervous. At least one thing is certain, I must be wearing the prettiest dress in the whole of Dragca. It's spectacular. My wedding dress is a deep blood red in colour, strapless and tight at the top before falling into a princess gown at the bottom. The top part is lacy, covered in red jewels that sparkle in the light, each one no doubt hand stitched on for this day. My hair curls down my shoulders in lovely waves, each one seeming perfect and soft to touch. Two dragon women came to help me with my dress and hair and makeup. They somehow have made me look dramatically more like a bride on her mating ceremony day, even if I am just a bundle of nerves.

I'm not nervous about mating with Kor. No, my soul knows that is the right thing for us because I love him. I'm nervous about mating in front of every dragon and seer here. I want to do my mother proud, but I so wish she were here to tell me what to do. How to act strong when you are truly scared. Dagan and Thorne are with Korbin, helping him get ready, and it strikes me that I don't have anyone around to help me. Melody and Hallie should be here, they should be my bridesmaids. My mother should be here, she should be doing my hair and whispering words of encouragement. I rub my heart, knowing I can't cry right now, but this dress is like having my mother with me in a way. I remember her letter, how she was proud of me even as a baby. I know deep down that she is proud of me in some way.

"One second," I manage to shout back before picking up the crown and placing it on my head. Now I look like a queen who is ready to mate with one of the loves of her life. Even if one of the other ones is in a dungeon and won't see me without causing me to break down. Every night for the past week, I've gone to see him, and he won't speak to me anymore, but he is eating at least. He looks better each time I see him, but still not my Eli.

I know I need to put thoughts of Elias away for now and enjoy this day with Korbin. A real mating ceremony. Not that I don't love how I mated to Dagan and Thorne, but I've always imagined a day like this. I pick up my dress to turn before dropping it and walking to my bedroom door, pulling it open. Essna is fixing my uncle's tie in his suit, tightening it up and putting it back into place. There is a moment when neither of them seems to notice I'm here, both of them staring at each other before the door creaks and they turn towards me. *That is interesting.*

"Right, you are all done. I will tell them to start in two minutes, Queen Isola," Essna says, dropping her hands from my uncle and bowing her head before very quickly walking away. My uncle watches her go, same as I do before he looks towards me. He bows his head before walking over.

"You look so similar to your mother on her wedding day, it almost hurts to see you if I am being honest. May I ask why you chose a red dress, ice queen?" he asks, stopping in front of me and offering his arm. I hook my arm in his just as I hear light music coming from the direction of the stairs. The music makes this all the more real.

"The same reason it was rumoured my mother wore a red wedding dress despite everyone telling her she should have worn blue or white," I say, listening to the sweet hum of the music that is romantic and deep in its meaning. "I wear this dress to show ice and fire dragons are one. It means nothing that I am ice, because I will always care for fire. This dress shows my respect for all dragons."

"She would be so proud of you on this day. Somewhere, your mother is watching, honoured by you," my uncle carefully says, and I have to swallow the emotions that nearly make me cry as we get to the top of the stairs. The music plays in the distance, the people are standing all around the stairs which have a white train down the middle, leading outside. There are white petals scattered everywhere, and lights on the edge of the staircase that give it a magical effect. It is beautiful in here, and I can't help but continue looking around at everything.

As we start walking down the staircase, snow starts falling from the ceiling, adding to the magic. I frown, wondering where the snow is coming from until I see Thorne standing next to Dagan by the door. They both look amazing, wearing black suits with red ties. The suits look almost custom fitted even though I know they had to go to Earth and buy a load of suits and dresses for the day because they didn't have time to have clothes made. The wedding preparations have given everyone a new sense of life, something to be happy about for even a few hours. I'm so glad we are doing this, not only for Kor and me, but for our people. I smile at the beauty, the magic of the perfect moment as I walk to my mates, and my uncle lets go of my arm when we are stood in front of them.

"Your current mates will deliver you to your new mate. It is what is right," my uncle says, kissing the side of my head. "I am ever so proud of the woman and queen you have become. Congratulations, Isola." His words make my voice catch as I nod at him, speechless before he steps back. At some point, Louis has become more of a father figure to me than my real father ever was. I link hands with Thorne and Dagan before we start to walk forward.

You are so beautiful, Dagan whispers into my mind.

Says you who looks so damn good in that suit, I reply, and

I hear his little chuckle just as I see Korbin at the end of the white path of petals outside. He is stood under a red- and blue-flowered arch placed in the middle of a star shape that is painted into the grass, his eyes widening before burning red as he sees me. My dragon purrs in my mind at the sight of him too. He is impressively attractive, dressed in a black suit and red tie, with a blue flower clipped into his breast pocket. We are silent as we walk past all the people watching us at the sides. I nod at Korbin's parents stood to one side, who both look so proud and emotional. His mother is crying, and I almost want to comfort her, but I know it is not the right time. I turn back to Kor, locking eyes with him as we get closer, and my mates let go of my hands. They stay right behind me as I take the final step, and Kor lifts one of my hands, kissing the back.

"You look beyond stunning, doll," he tells me, making my cheeks burn as red as my dress, I suspect. I go to say something back when a throat clears, and I turn to see a man I don't know stood behind the arch. He has my mating stone in his hand, a long white cloak with the hood up only showing me his dark red eyes and long black beard. I look at him for a moment, trying to figure out where I know him from when I suddenly realise he is a priest. There are few of them left in our world, or any of the worlds, and they only come out to bless a mating ceremony. It was rumoured a priest held my parents' ceremony, though it was not blessed.

"We gather here today for the royal mating ceremony of Isola Pendragon and Korbin

Dragoali," the man says, his voice echoing around as snow falls around us. "As we all know, mating is a blessing and something that cannot be taken for granted." There is silence as both Kor and I bow our heads in acknowledgement, knowing everyone here is doing the same thing. "Now speak the words." Kor turns to me, taking both my hands in his and holding them between us.

"Link to the heart, link to the soul. I pledge my heart to you, for you, for all the time I have left. My dragon is yours, my love is yours, and everything I am, belongs with you," he says, and I can't help the massive smile on my lips as I repeat the words, trying not to let my voice waver with how happy I am. When we can pull our eyes away, we see our mating stone is glowing brightly. Another blessed mating. We both offer the priest our hands as he pulls a dagger out. I hold in a cry as he cuts my hand and then cuts Kor's next.

"Light and dark, good and evil, and everything that makes us dragons, please bless this mating. We bless you," the priest says, and all the guests, all my people, join in echoing, "We bless you," as we place our cut hands together. The moment we touch, a massive blast of white light shines in every direction, sending off sparks of white dust that fall all around us as I grin at Kor.

I love you, my new mate, Kor whispers into my mind as his emotions flood me. Happiness, love and protectiveness are all I can feel for a long time.

I love you more, mate, I about manage to reply as tears fall down my cheeks just as the priest talks.

"Congratulations, you are one, and blessed by the fates. We bless you," the priest says as he starts fading away into white dust. Korbin pulls me into his arms, kissing me as everyone cheers.

CHAPTER 9

ISOLA

"You look so happy," Korbin whispers in my ear as we sway to the music in the courtyard. Dagan and Thorne have had a dance with me and made me laugh. Even my uncle has asked for a dance, though it was more formal, and from the way he looked at me, I know he was seeing my mother instead of me. That's okay though; it feels like part of her is here with me on this day. We have all had some delicious food, laughed, and Thorne even made a funny speech. This is a day I know I will never forget. Dagan and Thorne have gone back to watch Elias for the night to give Korbin and me some time alone. The music relaxes me, letting me sink into it as I hold my mate close.

"I'd be happier when you've taken me up to bed and completed our mating," I seductively whisper into his ear, making sure to brush my lips against them as I pull my head back to face him. His burning red eyes make it clear his dragon likes that idea. Kor gradually comes back, and he slowly kisses me, teasing me with every moment as the song ends. When he lets me go, he takes my hand and leads me out of the dancers and towards the building without saying a word. However, from the way I can sense his emotions, I know what is on his mind as it is on mine. I chuckle when he wraps an arm around my waist and pulls me close to him. I can sense the burning desire from our bond, and there is nothing more I want than to get upstairs with Kor and finish our bond.

We wave and say hello to people as we pass them, both of us just desperate at this point to get away from the number of people here. We hurry up the stairs together, both of us laughing with each other. We run to our room, and I push the door open. Kor closes it behind him and pulls me to him, kissing me like a starving man. I let out a little moan, holding onto him tightly as he pulls at my dress, and his lips press into my neck, nipping and biting gently. My dress rips at the back, and he pulls it off me as I undo his buttons on his shirt. My dress falls off me, leaving me just in red underwear as Kor steps back. He slowly pulls his tie off and then pushes his shirt off, revealing his toned chest, the dip in his lower chest and the six-pack. His hands go to his trousers, but I step closer, covering his hands with mine and stopping him.

"Let me, mate," I whisper before falling to my knees. I undo his trousers slowly, letting my fingers drift across his stomach, and enjoy the deep breath I hear him make every time I do it. I free his length before taking him inside my throat. He groans, holding onto my head and guiding my movements. It isn't long before he is picking me up off the floor and taking me to the bed. He throws me on it, and I bounce, laughing as he crawls over me. He kisses me harshly, pressing his body into mine, before he starts kissing his way down my body. Every kiss makes my skin tingle, makes me let out little gasps which turn into moans as his lips find my nipples. He takes his time sucking and twirling his tongue around each one, driving me crazy before he kisses down my stomach. The moment his tongue finds my core, I scream out the orgasm that slams into me along with the overwhelming desire coming from Kor through our bond. I gasp as Kor climbs up my body, locking eyes with me.

I love you more than I ever thought it was possible to love anyone, Isola. You are my mate, and we will be with each other forever, he speaks the breathtakingly sweet words into my mind as he slides deep inside me, making me moan out his name like a prayer.

I never knew either, but make me your mate. I love you, always, I reply. My words send Kor into a frenzy as he grabs my ass with one hand and holds the back of my neck with his other as he thrusts in and out of me. I can't help the noises that escape my lips with every thrust that pushes me closer to the edge. I cry out as another orgasm slams into me, and Kor kisses me deeply as he finishes too. He rocks into me a few more times, kissing me softly before rolling over. We hold hands, staring up at the ceiling of my room as we both calm down before we clean up. I sit on the window seat, looking over the courtyard. I should be happier than ever in this moment. I have three mates that I've been in love with since I met them. I have people who care about me, willing to fight a war I have made worse...yet my thoughts drift to Elias in the dungeons. I need to get him back, and nothing is going. to be right until I make a drastic move. I have to make him remember, no matter what.

CHAPTER 10

ISOLA

I wait until Kor has drifted into a deep sleep before climbing out of the bed and pulling on some clothes. I clip my cloak on before walking to the door, pausing to look over at Kor, and making sure my emotions are as neutral as I can get them before leaving the room. If any of my mates sense how scared I am to do this, they will know something is wrong and come to me. I can't even feel guilt, instead I try to make myself remember how resolved I need to be. I very slowly open the door and close it before walking down the empty corridors, each one of my steps echoing.

The party is long over, and the academy is happily sleeping after the celebrations, which is why I need to do this right now. I realised as I lay with Kor that nothing could be perfect until I sort out Eli. He has to remember me. I need him back in my life.

I freeze in the corridor when I hear footsteps and quickly step back into the shadows of a corner, holding my breath as two dragons stumble past me, laughing and stinking of beer. I wait until they are gone before walking to the top of the stairs, looking around to see it's empty before I run down the stairs and around the corner. I walk straight up to the two unfamiliar guards stood outside the dungeon doors. They bow when they see me, and I place a finger against my lips when one of them goes to speak.

"Are Dagan or Thorne down there?" I quietly ask.

"Dagan is, but Thorne left to help Essna with a border issue," one of them states, and that is perfect for me.

"Okay, I need you both to go to Dagan and tell him there is a big issue at the border. That you will watch Elias for him until his return," I say, and they look at me with confusion, no doubt going to argue, but I beat them to it. "That is an order from your queen. You will not tell Dagan anything about me being here either."

"Yes, our queen," they finally say and bow their heads before opening the doors. I run to hide under the stairs, keeping my emotions as tucked away as I can as Dagan walks out the dungeons, talking with the guards before storming off towards the doors of the academy. I wait for a few moments before walking out of my hiding space and to the doors.

"Thank you," I say, walking between them and looking back as they go to follow me into the dungeon. "No, stop."

"Queen, we only wish to protect you," they say, looking between each other with equal amounts of worry. I hate to boss them around when they are only doing the right thing, but it is important they don't stop what I am about to do. Though it might be easier to get the keys off them while I'm being bossy anyways.

"I am your queen, and I will tell you what to do. Now give me the keys to the cell and then wait outside. Whatever you hear, you do not come in here," I say, holding my hand out. They look between each other before one of the guards pulls out the key from his pocket and hands it to me. I take the key and raise my eyebrow, waiting for them to turn around, and I shut the doors before walking down the steps.

"I didn't expect to see you on your mating day, princess," Elias taunts as I get to the bottom step and see him resting on the side wall of the cage, crossing his arms. I run my eyes over his pale skin and dark eyes that match his black hair. This is now or never. I don't have time or a choice anymore. Eli must remember, even if what I'm going to do might kill us both.

"I had to do this. I'm tired of playing this cat and mouse game with you, Eli. You are mine, and you will remember me," I state, keeping my voice firm as I walk straight up to the cage. His eyes widen as I unlock the door, pulling it open and stepping inside. I leave the door open and chuck the key on the ground before standing right in front of Eli who watches me like the cat I know he is. Though he just doesn't know I am his equal in every way, and I will never run from him again.

"That was a bad move, naughty princess," he finally says and pushes up off the bars to walk closer to me. I stay very still as he places both his hands on my cheeks and moves his face inches away from mine.

"Nothing I do to save you is a bad move, Eli," I reply, gulping as his hands slide down my face and to my neck. I'm not shocked when he spins us around, pushing me against the bars as he tightens his hands on my neck. It's a half-assed attempt to kill me, because deep down, I know he doesn't want to. He knows it too, but he is so lost in the darkness, he can't tell me that. He keeps tightening his hands until I feel like I can't breathe anymore, but instead of panic, there is just acceptance that if he can kill me, he never truly loved me. I'd die to test what I am sure of.

His hands tighten further, and I grab his arms as my dragon roars in my mind, begging me to fight for my life, but I won't. Just as black spots enter my vision, tears fall down his cheeks, and I know I have to say something, do something before I pass out and can't. I call my light in the way I have prac- tised, and it blasts out of me in swirls that twirl themselves around Eli. I see the light out of the corners of my eyes, but I can't look away from him as he lifts me off the ground, putting more pressure on my neck.

"E-Eli...k-kill me if that is what you n-need to re- remember." His hands loosen on my neck slightly at my coughed out words, just as the light blasts to fill the entire room. For the first time in weeks, he looks at me like he remembers us as the light fades, and a hope fills my heart.

"Isola?" he whispers my name, dropping his hands and falling to his knees with a scream as he holds his head. I fall to the floor, gasping for air as the door blasts open, and I feel Dagan running in with Thorne and Korbin not far behind. I crawl to Eli, taking his face in my hands as he lies passed out on the ground, whimpering in pain. *Did I hurt him?*

"Isola, what were you thinking?" Dagan asks, falling to his knees and picking me up as I keep coughing.

"I saved him," is all I can manage to whisper before I pass out.

CHAPTER 11

DAGAN

I step out of Isola's room as the healer follows me, and I go to my brother's side. The healer says they will both recover, though she cannot tell if Eli is back to himself. I only have what Isola said to go on before she passed out. Thorne and Kor are staying with Isola as she recovers from almost being strangled to death by Elias. I don't know what went through her pretty little mind when she decided to risk her life to save my brother, but I know it comes from pure love. I just hope it actually worked and wasn't for nothing.

I shut the door to Elias's room as the healer leaves and pull a chair over to the side of his bed, looking down at my brother who I don't recognize anymore. I would do anything to save him, anything but lose Isola which we came too close to doing tonight. My brother is deep down inside of this shell somewhere, and he is in love with her, that is the only reason she is actually alive, I suspect.

The door opens once again, and I turn with a frown to see who has come in here. Bee flies into the room, looking determined as she lands on Eli's chest with a massive bag of glittering dust in her arms. She drops the dust all over Elias, and it spreads over all his skin as I step back.

"Bee, what was that?" I ask her in shock. Eli starts looking better almost instantly, colour coming back into his cheeks, and his hair looking softer.

"Fix him. Want back," she says and starts glowing brightly as I'm just relieved to see her back with us. Bee should be protected, not out in the world alone like she was. When Isola wakes up, at least she'll be happy Bee is back, even if Eli isn't himself.

"Have you fixed him then?" I ask her, needing to try to understand what is going on.

"For now," she says, nodding her head, and her eyes drift towards the door to Isola's room.

"Isola misses you. You should see her," I gently suggest. I know Isola has been worrying about Bee as much as she has been scared for Eli. I can only hope that at least seeing Bee will make her better when she wakes up.

"Must find more. I be back soon," she says, her voice sad and full of longing for Isola, no doubt. She flies out the room before I can even reply, leaving me more worried for her. It's clear she is trying to save Eli for Isola, even if it likely isn't safe for her. I will explain this all to Isola later. I look back as Eli groans, rolling onto his side before blinking his eyes open. We left the collar on him just in case he tries to attack us, though from the way he looks at me, I suspect Isola might have been right.

"Brother?" Eli asks, and I come closer, putting my hand on his shoulder. He doesn't push me away, so that is a good sign.

"You remember me? Do you remember Isola?" I ask him, watching his expression closely.

"You should kill me for what I said to Isola. For nearly killing her," he whispers, his voice filled with so much embarrassment and pain that I only want to fix it all for him, though I can't this time.

G. BAILEY

"Brother, if you were anyone else, under any other circumstances, you would be dead already. I know you didn't mean it and you love her," I tell him. "Isola knows the same."

"I do love her. I've really fucked up," he mutters, the guilt clear in his voice. "I will fix it, however I can. I never did deserve her, this just proves it."

"None of this is your own making, so stop with the guilt shit and get angry. Tatarina killed you, turned you into this monster to hurt Isola because she knew how much you mean to Isola. Now we will get revenge and live a damn happy life all together afterwards. Got it?" I wait for him to nod, a single tear falling down his cheek. I haven't seen my brother cry since our mother died. The simple fact this is all so fucked up for him kills me. "Good. Now, do you want to sit up?" He nods in agreement, his expression showing he's clearly still in some pain. I help him sit in the bed, pushing himself up on the pillows before I get him some water from the sink in the room. He sips on it for a bit as I glance at him again.

"You look better already," I muse, seeing that he isn't as pale as he once was, and his eyes have a little blue in them that was not there before, "though I'm going to get you some food in a bit. That should help."

"Any chance of a cigarette while you're at it?" he cheekily asks.

"Now I know you are back," I reply, laughing with him.

"You've always been looking after me, haven't you?" he says, and I guess he is right in a way. One of the last things I remember my mother telling us was to look after my brother, and it stuck around, even when he was being a dickhead until he met Isola.

"You're my brother. It's what we do," I reply, chuckling as his expression goes dark as he gets lost in his own thoughts.

"I still hear Tatarina in my head, whispering thoughts and demands to me. Whatever Isola did, it didn't completely work," he carefully tells me.

"Bee is helping too. We will fight this. We will fight her," I tell him, hating how vulnerable he looks for a moment as he meets my eyes.

"Kill her. Promise me no matter what, you will kill her," he asks.

"She is bonded to you," I whisper back, shaking my head. "I would be killing you if I did that."

"I know the price, but Isola needs to be queen. She needs Tatarina dead, and I will pay that price for her. Promise me, brother," he asks, and I know there is a good chance I will regret the next words. They upset me more than I thought words could possibly damage me as I speak them.

"I promise I will kill her if I get a chance. For Isola, and for you."

CHAPTER 12

ISOLA

"*C*ome to me, I will let you go if you do, Isola. This war is between me and you, no one else," a dark, mysterious voice whispers to me as I open my eyes to see the fire I am stood in the middle of. There is nothing but fire all around as I twist, trying to find the familiar voice.*

"*How can I come to you if I don't know who you are or how to find you?*" I ask, searching for the voice.*

"*You may have saved that boy of yours, but one touch from me and he will be mine again. Come to me, and I will leave him alone. He still will die if you kill me,*" I freeze in my spot, knowing exactly who is talking to me from the threat alone. Good, I want her to know my thoughts.*

"*Eli is mine, and you will never have him. Oh Tatarina, I*

*will come for you, but you won't want me there, because it
will be the day I kill you. I will make sure Dragca forgets
your name, and you will be nothing but a bad memory. I will
come for you, but you should run for what you have done," I
reply, kneeling down and reaching inside my heart for my
light. Bright white light blasts out of my chest, putting out the
fire as I hear Tatarina screaming. I smile just as I fall back
into the safe darkness of my dreams.*

I gasp as I wake up, sitting straight up as the
light of the room burns against my eyes as I
remember Tatarina being in my dreams. She
knows Eli is mine now, and that means there is no
reason why she won't be heading our way with her
army. I must tell Essna and my uncle, though
knowing them, they already have come to that
conclusion. I reach for my throat, feeling how
tender it is just before a glass of water appears in
front of me. I accept it and down the drink before
looking up to see who gave it to me and nearly
cough the water out. *Eli.* My Eli is sat on my bed,
his eyes riddled with guilt as he takes the empty
glass off me, our fingers brushing each other's
before he places it on the side. He looks better,
healthier than he ever has, and all I can do is stare.

It really worked, and he is here, smelling of smoke but missing the smirk I'm used to seeing on his lips. His collar is gone, so clearly my mates trust him with me. I'm so happy, I feel like I can't even breathe.

"I'm so, so fucking sorry for every shitty word that came out my mouth recently. I will never be able to tell you how sorry I am for hurting you," he admits, looking away from me and down to his hands, no doubt reliving that moment in the dungeon.

"I knew it wasn't you," I say, my voice coming out croaky as I reach out and take his hand in mine, brushing my fingers across the rough skin. "I knew you were hidden deep down inside somewhere."

"Tatarina killed me...I remember it," he tells me, his voice is quiet though, and my dragon roars to life in my mind, letting out a whine as snow starts to fall from the ceiling. Eli doesn't take his eyes off me as it falls around us, he only stares at me like he expects me to hate him.

"I wish I could have stopped her from doing that to you, but she will pay," I vow. "I will find a way to make sure you have a long life…with me."

"I'm still linked to her. I hear her in my head, but

Bee keeps doing this light thing that makes me better and her voice goes. Though she can't keep doing it," he admits. "If things go bad, lock me up again."

"That is never happening, and she isn't the only one that can use light to heal you. Wait, Is Bee is back?" I ask, reaching up a hand and placing it on his cheek.

"Was she ever gone?" he asks, and I remember that he doesn't know anything that happened when we went to Earth and came back here. I know I need to catch him up soon.

"Yes, she was. She disappeared when we came back from Earth. Where is she?" I ask him.

"She's been outside with Dagan, Korbin and Thorne since she came back again with some more dust last night. You've been out two days from whatever you did to make me remember."

"I used light, but it was different. I didn't want to give up until you looked at me like this," I say, sighing as I move a little closer to Eli on the bed.

"I'm just glad we get some moments before the war. I missed you, my naughty princess," he gently says, picking up a little bit of my hair and twirling it around his fingers.

"I missed you—the real you—so much Eli," I say, and he lets me climb onto his lap, wrapping my arms and legs tightly around him. The moment his arms hold me tightly, I let out a sigh of relief. I have just wanted him to hold me since all this happened.

"So...you don't hate me?" he quietly asks. "I can handle *anything* but you hating me." I slide my hands onto his cheeks, seeing how vulnerable he looks because he's hurting.

"I could never hate you. *Never*. I love you an impossible amount, and I'm nothing but happy you are back with me. We will figure forever out and win the war, but for now I just want to be near you," I tell him, breathing in his smoky scent as I look back to see his eyes. There is a bit of the dark blue I love in there but mainly his eyes are still so dark, the blackness getting in. I can get used to it as long as I have Eli. Nothing else matters.

"I will spend whatever time I have making sure nothing ever happens like that again," he promises, and then he finally kisses me. The first moment our lips touch, I only feel how cold he is and yet how perfect he feels. I slide my hands into his hair as I deepen the kiss, and he pulls me closer to him. I rock against him, just wanting to be as close as possible to my Eli, and he lets out a little groan.

"God, I love you," I whisper between kisses, not being able to stop smiling with how damn happy I am. He goes to say something when there is a loud shout somewhere nearby and then a blaring alarm reaches our ears as I pull away from Eli. Seconds later the door blasts open with Dagan running in through it.

"You need to see this, Isola," Dagan states as I climb off the bed and follow him out of the room, down the corridor which is full of running people who don't even notice us, and he stops, pulling a door open to a balcony. I walk out, looking over at the trees with Dagan and Eli at my sides. There are moving slightly, and the sound of a lot of people heading our way fills my ears.

"Is it Tatarina's army?" I ask Dagan, knowing it is very likely that it is.

"I don't know. You should stay here while we investigate," Dagan warns, and I smirk at him before climbing on the balcony wall and jumping off as I shift into my dragon, and I hear him and Eli swear in annoyance. I fly across the grounds, seeing people ducking below me before I land right on the edge of the forest. I breathe out a wall of ice, leaving only a little gap right in front of me to see who is coming through.

No, danger... my dragon hisses before letting me shift back. I stand still, crossing my arms as I hear my army and mates running towards me just as a familiar face steps out of the tree line first.

"Queen Isola, I heard you need our help."

CHAPTER 13

"Queen Winter...what are you doing here?" I question her as she looks at the walls of ice and walks through the gap. Four men stay close to her side, all of them no doubt her mates from the scent of them. I see a woman stood in the front of the army, dressed in all leather with a giant sword on her back and a brown haired man stood close to her side. Though Winter is dressed similarly in a black leather outfit and her long brown hair is up in a bun, she doesn't seem as intimidating as the other girl is. I pull my eyes from her to the four men that walk over with Winter. One is an angel with big white wings that match his hair. I nod my head at Atticus, but I do not know the other two. One smells like a dog though, so I'm thinking he is the wolf that stayed close to Winter's side but wouldn't shift back.

Very slowly, my ice melts as I lift a hand, revealing a big army that stands behind them just in the tree line. All their scents mix together, so I can't really get a read on what they are. Just that they look like an army. I search for my sister, but I don't get to see her before Winter steps in front of me and starts speaking as she crosses her arms. I feel Kor step to my side, his arm brushing mine as Dagan gets to my other side. I sense Thorne close, but he isn't here yet. I'm sure Eli is on his way as well. My heart feels complete, even for a moment as I watch the Earth queen for answers. I have my men at my side, all of them, and that means I can handle anything.

"Did you really think I wasn't going to come to the world of dragons when you needed my help?" Winter asks, a small smile on her lips. I feel that instant connection with her again, and I don't know what it is, but it makes me want to trust her. I do trust her, even if I don't know much of Winter at all. I move my eyes to her four mates, who are all staring in awe at the dragons flying around the castle. The army behind her all look just as shocked.

"This fight won't be easy. We could all die," Korbin warns from my side.

"I know, dragon, but we won't let Dragca fall. Just like I assume you won't let Earth fall either if we ever need you. We are all linked by fate, and I know I am meant to be here. I know I am fated to fight by queen Isola's side."

"This is a dragon war, I don't want you hurt in it," I admit to her.

"I can handle myself, much like we all can. I would not come if I wasn't sure you would need us. After Melody explained..." she drifts off, confirming my fear that Melody is here when she should not be. It isn't safe for her, she told me so herself.

"Where is she?" I ask.

"Coming soon. The army is rather large, and she had to come through last with her girlfriend," she claims. I look around the army, wondering if they will even stand a chance in a dragon fight. Wolves, angels, vampires and witches don't belong in a dragon fight. I guess I have to trust they are stronger than they look.

"It is your choice, my queen," Dagan says as I look up at him for a bit of advice.

"We need help. They know the price they could pay," I reply to him, placing my hand on his arm and looking back to Winter. "If you want to help us win this war, we will happily accept. I will also personally owe you a great debt. If Earth ever needs help, we will answer the call," I tell her, and she smiles, offering me her hand to shake. I slide my hand into hers, and we shake on it before she pulls me into a tight hug.

"I'm your friend first, and I will never let a friend die if I didn't try to help her. Now show me this dragon world you are from as our mates sort the army out," she tells me, and I chuckle as I pull away.

"I'd love that," I reply and look towards Kor and Dagan.

Can you help sort out the army into rooms and anything they need? I ask through our bond.

"Of course," they both reply, before going over and introducing themselves to Winter's mates as Winter and I walk away. Most of my people bow, looking a little confused at the new army, but they all walk over as we pass them. It's about time Dragca's people find out we aren't alone nor the only supernaturals in the worlds.

"This is Dragca Academy, though it isn't in use at the moment. We used to use it as a school for most dragons as they came into their powers," I explain to Winter as she looks up at what is left of Dragca Academy. It's broken in places, but the main part of the castle is intact.

"You know, that is what I want in our home. It is also a castle, very similar to this one with a protection ward. I want it to be a place all of our kind can send their children to learn to control their gifts. Maybe when this war is over and we have peace, we could work together to set up a Supernatural Academy. One that mixes all of our people. What do you think?" she asks, and as I look at her, I can see our future. All our people travelling freely between Dragca and Earth. Our children growing up together, being friends as they eventually take our thrones.

"It sounds like a future worth fighting for, Winter," I eventually reply, and I can see she is thinking the same thing as I am as we both look back at the castle as we get closer.

"It does, doesn't it?" she says.

"How is Jonas?" I ask her, wanting to know about the boy I think of every so often. I feel like I owe the memory of Jace a debt, and I will look after his brother no matter what.

"Happily running around the castle. He and the other dragons have been helping us re-build some damaged houses," she tells me, and I smile in relief. "My best friend Alex has adopted one of the dragon boy babies we found. She asked me to ask you if it was alright if she looked after him permanently with her mate, Drake."

"Of course. Though when he is older, he might need some dragon training here," I suggest. "I'm glad to know one of the babies has found a family."

"Yes, me too. If anyone can handle a dragon son, it's Alex. She knows he will need to return to his home one day, but she and Drake felt an instant bond with him," Winter explains to me. "He is the cutest baby though. All that white hair that is like snow, and deep ruby red eyes."

"Then he has found a home. I was brought up on Earth and lived happily there," I explain to her so she knows dragons can live on Earth with no problem.

"I didn't know what I was for many years. I grew up with a human mother, went to human schools until I found my stepson hurt in a car park, and my story began," she tells me, which I didn't expect to hear.

"Maybe more than fate links us, perhaps our upbringing is something that links us also. Just think, we are both queens who grew up in normal schools just like any human," I say, with a chuckle as she smiles in agreement. We get to the stairs, and Essna comes down the steps with my uncle at her side. They both bow before lifting their heads.

"I believe we might finally have a chance now that your friend is here. We welcome the Earth queen to Dragca Academy and wish your first time here wereunder better circumstances," Essna formally says.

"This is Essna, leader of the seers, and my uncle, Louis," I introduce them to Winter. They all shake hands and exchange small nods.

"My mate, Dabriel, is very interested in learning more about seers. He believes they are very connected with their similar gifts somehow. Though he believes we are all children of fates and tied to each other in some ways we will never understand," Winter says.

"I believe a chat with your mate would be very interesting for me as well. We are children of the ancient fates. It is said they breathed life into Dragca, creating both dragons and seers, though no one sees the fates anymore to find out the truth," Essna says, and I share a little look with Winter, both of us have a tiny smile on our lips.

"Essna, we should go and introduce our people," Louis says, gently touching her arm before dropping his hand like she burnt him or something. Her cheeks are a little red as she nods, and they both bow to us before walking away.

"Is it me, or is there some sexual tension there?" Winter whispers as we carry on walking up the steps.

"It's not just you, but my uncle is complicated and lost. I'm sure if anyone could find him, it could be a seer like Essna," I quietly say as we step through the doors, and I see Bee flying through the air towards me with a big smile.

"Oh no, Bee. Where the hell have you been?" I demand, and she pauses with a guilty look.

"I had to fix," she says, and as much I suspect she was finding the dust to fix Elias, I still could have lost her.

"Fix what? Why couldn't you tell me you were going to leave? Let me help you? You have no idea how worried I have been about you! Don't you ever run off in a war again without talking to me, Bee," I say, telling her off, and she nods, flying a little closer and resting her head on my shoulder as I rub her back, holding her close.

"I'm sorry. I had to fix," she mumbles, and I sigh, wiping away a tear as Winter looks at us both, tugging on her rucksack on her back.

"I'm sorry I shouted. I love you, Bee. I can't lose you. Ever," I whisper to her. I was only mad because the idea of anything happening to Bee makes me want to tear the world apart.

"We are one. No lose, but must save Nane. She sister," she whispers into my ear, and I look at her eyes.

"I know, I just don't know how to save her. Yet."

"*W*hat the bloody hell is that?" Eli asks, and I turn to look down the corridor just as a blue blur of a creature slams straight into my chest, knocking me to the ground. I cough, lifting the blue creature that looks like a mini troll with strange clothing on into the air.

"MILO!" Winter shouts down the corridor as the small creature—who I assume is called Milo—grins at me before flying out of my hands into the air and making a quick exit in the opposite direction of Winter's room where I just left her. Eli and I were going to find Melody and Hallie to see why they are actually here. Bee went to make a tree in my room to sleep in tonight. I know I need to send Melody home as soon as possible, so I left Bee to it. Melody said coming back to Dragca before the war was over could kill her, and I won't lose my sister for anything in the entire world. Winter, seeming flustered, comes running out the room, looking around before getting to Eli and me.

"Did you see a little blue demon anywhere around?" she asks, and I point down the corridor.

"Wait, did you say demon?" I ask with wide eyes. *Demons are real?*

"Yes, a silly little demon who snuck into my bag when I told him not to come here. I swear, he is worse than Freddy and Josh about following goddamn rules," Winter mutters, not that I have clue who they are, before she storms off down the corridor. I don't want to be Milo when she finds him. Eli pulls me close to his side as I whisper to him.

"Demons, angels and god knows what else we have in the Dragca Academy. I literally could never have predicted this for my future," I say, and he laughs.

"Even if they ride in here with flying unicorns, I

don't care. Whatever help we can get to win the war is important," he gently tells me, making me chuckle before he kisses me.

"Hello, sis. I'm glad to see you fixed your last mate as war is coming swiftly," Melody's sweet voice comes to us as I break away from Eli and turn to see her and Hallie walking over. They both have long blue cloaks on and are covered in daggers and swords. Melody's orb is resting on a staff I've never seen before, it looks like it is made of literal gold. I run over to Melody, hugging her tightly as she holds me back before letting her go so I can hug Hallie.

"I'm glad to see you both," I say honestly, before stepping back and pulling my eyes to Melody, "though you said you couldn't come here because it would kill you."

"Futures change, and I need to be here," she tells me, though I sense she is lying to me a little as she doesn't keep eye contact.

"Promise me that I won't lose you and you're not lying to me because you know I will send you back, Melody?" I ask, taking her hands in mine, and she squeezes my hands tightly.

"I will do whatever it takes to save you and Dragca. Trust me, this is the only way," she replies, avoiding my question like seers do best. I will just have to keep Melody close to me. Or get help from my guys and lock her up somewhere safe when the war comes. Either option sounds safe...kinda.

"I won't lose you," I tell her, even if it feels like I lost her the moment she stepped into Dragca for me, and we both know it.

"I'll try not to die. Now aren't congrats in order? You have a new mate," Melody says, quickly changing the subject, as I glance at Hallie who I can tell is upset, but she is silent.

"Yes, I do," I reply as Eli says hello to them both.

"I will go and help the others and leave you with your sister and Hallie for a bit," Eli suggests, his hand resting on the middle of my back.

"Are you sure you are going to be alright?" I ask Eli, stepping away from my sister before he turns away.

"I'm okay. I will come and see you later. Enjoy your time with your sister and friend," he says, and I kiss him lightly before he leaves. I feel like we haven't gotten much time together since he has become himself, and there is still so much I want to talk to him about, but I know it isn't the time.

"Come on, let's find you guys a room and some drinks," I say as Hallie and Melody step to either side of me, and I enjoy the time I have with them.

CHAPTER 15

ISOLA

"*M*ilo does what?" I ask between breathless laughs, not really being able to stop myself laughing with the others as I sit with Melody, Hallie and Winter in the library in front of a roaring fire. This woman, Leigha, is here too, though she doesn't speak much and never takes off the scary swords she carries around like purses. She is Winter's guard in a way and believes it's her personal job to make sure Winter is safe. So she is standing by the door and refuses to sit with us in case there is any danger. Which doesn't make any sense as Essna boosted Dabriel's gifts with a power exchange, and he saw that Tatarina will fly with her army here in two nights' time. These are our last two nights together before war comes, and I plan to spend it with my guys and my sister.

The guys are checking out the weapon rooms before going to get us food, so Winter has been telling us stories about her little demon friend. He is a good demon, a breed which usually just likes to cause chaos on Earth when they escape Hell. Milo is currently hanging out with Bee since they like each other as they share marshmallows they are toasting on sticks in the fireplace before eating them.

"Yeah, it was a sight I don't think I could forget," Winter says with a little shudder.

"Hopefully he doesn't teach Bee any tricks," I chuckle, leaning back in my seat and looking at my sister who is cuddling Hallie. They look so perfect together. So happy, lost in themselves.

"I'm sure he will, and I'm sorry in advance," Winter chuckles, before sipping on her hot chocolate. I glance behind my seat when I hear a creak of a floorboard and see the old librarian standing near a window. I remember speaking to her not long after coming to Dragca Academy, and if I remember right, she spoke about curses and seemed to know a lot about them. Maybe she might know about light and dark magic.

"I will be right back," I tell them, hearing them muttering okay as I get up and walk over to the librarian.

"Hey, do you remember me?" I ask her, as I can't remember her name off the top of my head. The librarian turns towards me and bows her head.

"Princess Isola, now Queen. My name is Windlow Pakdragca as I can see you have forgotten," she tells me, and I lean against the window, looking out at what she was staring at. Angels fly around the perimeter, dragons above them going in the opposite direction. Not long after, wolves in a small pack walk past. One man stands still at the edge of the forest, and there is one in every direction as their sense would alert us to any change.

"It is strange to see all these different supernaturals all working together to stop a world being destroyed, isn't it?" I ask her, looking back as she watches me closely.

"It is not so strange but humbling to see we are not alone. You are a true queen, much like your mother. Though she made the ultimate sacrifice for her people," she says, and I run my eyes over her in confusion.

"What do you mean?" I ask her.

"She married a monster, willingly, because she knew you had to be born. You had to exist in such a dark world," she says, her voice tinged with sadness. "That was her cost, but then she was rewarded with you and knowing you will save the world she loved so dearly. Not just save but improve. The people will thrive with you as their queen."

"Did you know my mother? How could you possibly know this?" I ask her, but she pulls her eyes from me and towards the window.

"I comforted your mother at times. I was the royal librarian, and books were always a good escape in her eyes," she explains to me.

"The more I hear of my mother, the more I realise how alike we are. I only wish I had more time with her, found a way to save her," I admit.

"Don't we all wish we had more time with those we love?" she asks and crosses her arms. "Now, what did you want to speak to me about, my queen?"

"I wanted to know if you had any knowledge on

light and dark magic? On their spirits possibly?" I ask, and she nods.

"I know you need to make sure Nane is bonded to you before Tatarina dies. If she dies first, Elias Fire will die with her before you can bond with Nane," she informs me, and my lips part, the only movement I feel like I can make.

"Wow, you know more than I expected," I say with wide eyes.

"I know Elias Fire is bound to Nane, the dark magic she possesses brought him back to life. Tatarina may have used the magic, but it does not belong to her. Much like your light magic doesn't belong to you either, it is borrowed from Bee, and you can use it. If you bond with Nane, then you will be able to save the boy," she says, and then starts coughing out smoke as old dragons sometimes do. I push away from the window to go help her, but she waves a hand. "Return to your family and friends, this time is for you and them."

"Thank you for your help. You will go and rest now, though, right?" I ask her, and she nods, still coughing smoke.

"My time is near, but not yet. You can repay me for

my knowledge one day by taking me to the royal libraries. I do miss the books that live there very much," she tells me.

"I promise," I say, before bowing my head in a respectful way before walking back to my friends and family. Just as I get closer, Melody sees me and sighs in a nervous way before standing up. She offers her hands to Hallie, who smiles at her before letting Melody help her stand up.

"Right, well, everyone is here that I wanted, and I'm more nervous than I thought was possible to ask now," Melody says as she lets go of Hallie's hands, and starts searching her cloak pockets. Hallie gives me a look as I rest against Winter's chair, and I shrug my shoulders. I have no clue what Melody is doing. My eyes widen as Melody drops to one knee, holding out a ring with a large blue gemstone in the middle that reflects the firelight. The ring is stunning, and I hold my hand over my mouth as I realise what is happening.

"Hallie, I have dreamed of you—literally—for years until I got lucky enough to meet you, and you turned out to be a million times better than any dream. I know for certain that you are my future, and I love you so much. So, will you mate with me?

Marry me?" she asks, and I feel like we all hold our breath until Hallie nods and jumps into Melody's arms, kissing her as they fall to the floor. Winter and I clap and hug them both when they get up off the floor and get the ring on Hallie's hand.

"So, will you be my maid of honour and secretly attend our mating tonight? I only want a small ceremony with close family and friends," Hallie asks me, and I nod, hugging her tightly before pulling away.

"And mine too." Melody adds in, and I chuckle as I nod my head.

"Right, I'm going to find my dragons and get a ceremony sorted. Want to help, Winter?" I ask her, and she quickly gets up off her seat to follow me out of the room, neither of us can stop smiling the whole time.

CHAPTER 16

ISOLA

I clip the final slide into Melody's hair before stepping back and looking at the lovely hair design I've managed to help do. The top half is up in a braid, leaving the rest falling down her shoulders. I've clipped in little white flower slides we found, and overall, she looks so pretty.

"All done," I say, and she stands up, the white dress we managed to find on short notice fitting her perfectly. It's one that is tight all the way down her body, showing off her figure, and strapless at the top.

"Thank you, sis," she says, and then suddenly hugs me tightly, and I hear her little sobs only a moment later as I hold her close.

"I know you think you are going to die, and that's why you want to mate tonight. So that if you die, Hallie will have a good memory," I whisper, understanding my sister more than I even want to. It's something I would do and want to do. I don't know if Eli wants that with me yet, but I can only hope he does.

"How do you know that?" she quietly asks.

"I know you, sis. That is the same thing. I see the fear in your eyes every time we discuss the war. Every time someone speaks Tatarina's name," I reply, my voice a whisper.

"The future can change...that is what I'm hoping for, at least," she explains to me.

"You will not die. I won't let it happen," I tell her firmly.

"If I do, you promise you will look after Hallie?" she asks, and I nod, though I can see she knows I would anyways.

"No more talk of death tonight. We worry about it tomorrow night when we know it will be coming to our doors," I tell her, and she smiles, wiping her cheeks.

"Okay. I know you are right," she agrees. This is a night for celebration, not a night to be scared of what will come either way.

"Come on then, let's go and get your bride," I say, holding my arm out. Melody slides her arm into mine before we walk to the door, and I pull it open before we go out. We walk down the corridor in silence before Melody stops suddenly, and I jolt as I stop with her. "Cold feet?" I joke, and she shakes her head.

"I know telling you your future is risky and could make it worse, but I have to warn you. I feel like it is the right thing to do," she says, and I go to stop her saying anything when she starts speaking. "When Elias goes to kill Tatarina, you must duck as she shoots a bolt of ice at you, otherwise you will die." Her words seem to wrap around my throat until I nod, and we carry on walking to her wedding like nothing happened. I know it was a big risk for her to tell me this, but I know I don't have a choice now but to listen to what she just told me. Though Eli can't kill Tatarina until I get to Nane, that is too important.

We walk into the library where we have set up an alter and Windlow has agreed to perform the ceremony. There are rose petals sprinkled across the floor, and my mates with Eli are stood at the one side, and on the other is Winter and her mates. We are all dressed up for the wedding. Luckily Winter fit into a beautiful blue dress we found, and I am wearing the red dress I once wore to a mating cere- mony when I first came to Dragca. I stop at the end, kissing my sister's cheek before letting her go to stand next to Eli, who wraps an arm around my waist. All my mates and Eli look amazing tonight, all dressed up in suits that complement them.

I watch my sister and Hallie repeat the sacred words while Windlow holds their mating stone which Hallie found earlier today outside her room. The stone glows a bright white as they cut their hands, and we all cheer as they kiss, completing their mating. I wipe a few tears away as I hug my sister and then Hallie before letting them go off as Eli holds me close.

"You look beautiful, kitty cat," Dagan says, using the nickname I haven't heard him call me in a long time as he takes my hands into his and kisses them. "You really do look amazing," he tells me.

"I'm afraid I need to steal your mates to carry on preparations for the war," Winter's mate, Wyatt, states as he steps over to us. Winter has left with her angel mate and the wolf, leaving us with Wyatt and Atticus.

"That's okay," I say, looking at Thorne, Dagan and Korbin who take turns kissing me before leaving with Wyatt and Atticus. Eli holds me close as they go before we walk quietly through the library.

"Do you remember when I first found you reading in here?" Eli asks, walking me down an aisle and to the sofa seat where he found me. We both sit down, and I cuddle up to his chest, playing with his buttons as I listen to his breathing.

"Yes. I remember you calling my book girly porn," I tease him, and he laughs.

"Well, it was," he replies. "Anyhow, I wanted to kiss you that night, but I knew I couldn't. It was the first time my dragon insisted you were his. He went on and on all night about you, and the moment he left my mind alone, I was still thinking about you."

"What you said to me that night about falling in love? You were right," I gently tell him, lifting my head to meet his gaze.

"I know, but you are much stronger than I ever

thought you were. You will not lose anyone, Isola," he tells me, and I crawl up him as he leans back, his dark eyes watching my every movement.

"Kiss me, Eli," I say, and he smirks, sliding his hands up my back ever so slowly.

"No, you kiss me, naughty princess," he replies, and I grin before leaning down and kissing him. The moment our lips meet, we crush them together and he pulls my hips down, rolling me against his hard length under me. I moan, knowing I don't want to wait as I rip Eli's shirt open, and then we are ripping each other's clothes off in the next moment. He never takes his eyes off me as he rips my dress off and kisses down my body as it falls to the floor. Eli lays me down on the sofa before easily sliding inside me, making my back arch from the pleasure and a moan escape my lips. He chuckles, placing his hand over my mouth and whispering in my ear as he thrusts in and out of me.

"Shh, now. You don't want anyone to hear us and interrupt," he whispers, and I bite down on his hand as he picks up speed. Each thrust sends me closer to the edge until I can do nothing but cry out as an orgasm slams into me, and Eli groans my name as he finishes a moment later. He holds me close as we stare at each other, and I place my hand on his cheek.

"I want to mate to you," I whisper.

"I know, princess, but I can't. Not until this war is over and I know you won't lose me. I can't do that to you, no matter how much I want to be selfish," he whispers, making my heart hurt because I know deep down he is doing the right thing.

"Okay, but promise we will mate when the war is over?"

"Yes, because I love you and want nothing more," he says and kisses me as a tear escapes my eye, making me more determined than ever to win this war and save my Eli.

CHAPTER 17

ISOLA

*B*lack smoke spins around my legs as I open my eyes, the smoke drifting off in every direction in swirls that look like strange vortexes all around me. I know instantly that this is Tatarina getting in my dreams, using whatever connection she can to mess with me. I'm not overly surprised she would play this trick right before the war. It seems like something she would do.

"Are you going to come out rather than hiding like a little child?" I ask, looking around and waiting to see her, though something seems off about the dream in general. It doesn't feel as strong as the last one. Only a few moments later, a shadow of dark smoke, looking like Tatarina without any features appears. "Are you not strong enough to really enter my dreams?" I ask her the question, but I know the answer anyway.

"Come to me. We can end this all without so many dragon deaths tomorrow," she purrs, and I have no idea why she is bothering to try and taunt me. Or scare me. Even if I came to her, she would send her army to kill mine. No, this is all a trick.

"No, not yet. Go and hide in the castle, all alone, until the war. I am done having you in my dreams," I shout, and the shadow runs at me, its arms in the air. I go to call my light when suddenly a blast of white light fills my vision, making me shut my eyes. When I open my eyes, I'm in a room filled with gold and jewels. I recognise this place as the cave where I mated with Thorne, where the strange woman who claimed to be a fate and Winter's aunt lived.

"Are you not going to say hello? Or can you not hear me? It has been a while since I pulled a dream, and I might not have gotten it quite right," the old woman muses from behind me, and I spin around, seeing her sitting on a chair, playing with some glittering gold string. She is knitting. How...well, weird.

"Hi, I can see and hear you. I'm just a little confused on the how you are in my dreams and why..." I reply to her, and she looks up at me, still knitting the gold string, though she doesn't have to look down at it as she does. I stare at the string for a *moment, feeling a strange pull towards it. Whatever it is, it isn't just string.*

"Oh, never mind that. We fate have strange gifts. How are you?" she asks me.

"I have a feeling you didn't bring me here to ask how I am," I reply, "though if you must know I am worried about war. Worried about a lot of things."

"Oh, I forget how impatient you all are. Right, right. I did not bring you here to ask how you are. Your emotions are clear to everyone," she tuts and sits back.

"Why then?" I ask, sliding my hand to the necklace I like to make myself forget I wear. It is clipped around my neck, the stone a constant reminder of the price my first born will pay.

"I wanted to put your mind at ease. I sense you are very troubled about bringing your daughter to me," she says. It's strange to talk about a child that doesn't even exist yet—and may never. Though this fate seems certain she will come into my life at some point, which fills me with a false sense of hope that we might win this war.

"Wouldn't anyone be worried? I don't know you or what you want," I reply, watching the old lady carefully. I can't see any similarities with Winter besides the blue eyes, though they might have shared the same hair colour once, who knows?

This woman is too wrinkled, her long hair grey, but she still has this beauty about her that Winter carries. There is just something about them.

"I asked for your daughter to come to learn her powers under my guidance. It is important, as she is to become a new fate. She will be the second child ever to inherit such a power since the old times, the other is yet to return to her lands to claim her powers. Your daughter's power is a gift from the magic of Dragca itself and must be looked after," she explains to me. "Much like a child from Frayan has been given a gift, and a child of the Earth queen will have one too. Power is given to those who can command it and bring about peace."

"That's all you want her for? To train her with this power?" I ask her, and she nods. I avoid the bit about other children getting powers. I will remember to tell Winter about that later though.

"Yes. Then she will return home, unite the lands with that boy..." she stops with a laugh that I don't get. "Oh, wait. I should not say that. It is what humans call a spoiler alert when someone speaks too soon and ruins the book or movie. Never mind, you will see one day." I shake my head at her, wishing she told me whatever she seems to know.

"Thank you for telling me this, it does help," I admit to her. "And thank you for ending my dream with Tatarina."

"The lost queen will not visit your dreams anymore, she does not have the power to do so. You must wake now. Until we see each other again, Queen Isola..." I gasp as the floor below me disappears, and I fall into darkness before I can even say goodbye.

I sit up as I wake, feeling strangely awake and alert like I've drunk a million energy drinks or something as I calm my breathing down, remembering the two dreams. I rub the necklace on my neck, knowing that I have nothing to fear for my child's future. She will be powerful. Though first off, we need to win this war before even thinking about children. I look down at my skin, seeing it glowing a little before it fades, and I rest back against my pillows, feeling restless. There is no doubt the fate sent me back with a little power boost of some sort.

I glance over at Eli, who is sleeping with Bee next to him on his pillow. They look cute together, and I don't want to wake either of them when I see the time on my clock on the wall. It's four in the morning, and I know I should still be sleeping. War is coming tonight and there won't be any more dreams until it is over. The fate was right about that. I have an idea what I can do with my spare energy though.

I quietly slide out of the bed and pull on my clothes before brushing my hair in the bathroom and freshening up. I silently leave my room and walk down the corridors, bowing at the random person I bump into here and there, who are walking around. The corridors feel cold, like there is a chill in the air that mixes in with the tension every person here is feeling. I hope they are spending these last hours with those who they love, saying goodbye just in case. Something I know I need to do.

I find the room I'm looking for and try to open the door, seeing that it is locked no matter what way I turn it. I jiggle the handle a few times before stepping back and looking around. I'm sure no one will care if I break the door handle to get in, and there is no one around anyways. I close my hand around the handle, calling my ice and freezing it until it cracks. I step back and kick the door, and it flies open, revealing the room that looks nothing like I remember it. The once beautiful flower- and plant-filled classroom is all dead now; nothing at all looks alive in it. I guess no one could look after it after the teachers were killed. I suspected as much, but it's still sad to see the room that was so alive now so dead.

I walk in the room and up to the tree, the only thing that doesn't look as bad as everything else in the room. I place my hand on the bark, which is cold to touch, before I close my eyes, blocking out the rotting smell that fills my nose, reminding me how little life there is left in here. I want to fix that. I call my light, sensing Bee sleeping upstairs as I do, and seconds later, I feel the light leaving me in waves. The light warms my hand up until it feels like it is burning, and I let go of the bark, opening my eyes to see the now healthy tree I'm standing under. Every branch is filled with bright green leaves that have purple veins on them. The tree feels happy, if that it is even possible.

I look down at my shoes, seeing the soft looking grass under them and sighing. This is why I love light magic. I reach up and pick a pod off the tree, opening it up to find the sweet I know is inside from my old lessons here. It feels like honouring the memory of my teacher and of Dragca Academy by fixing this room. I crunch the sweet in my mouth, enjoying the blast of sweetness as I walk out of the branches. I stop in the middle of the room which is now full of bright, dazzling flowers that make my heart a little happier than it already was. Nature can be the most beautiful thing in the world sometimes, and I fixed this all.

I walk around, touching and smelling some of the flowers before leaving the room and deciding it might be a good idea to have a run outside to burn off more energy. I know it's dark out, but the darkness isn't that bad when there are guards all around the area. I walk to the main doors, pausing when I see Kor and his mother hugging outside the doors. His mother has a letter in her hand as she cries, and I feel Kor's pain through our bond now that I'm closer. I want to know what has happened, but I also don't want to interrupt their moment.

"Isola," Kor says, letting his mum go as he clearly senses me. I know I can't walk away and leave them to it now, so I go over, taking his hand in mine as I look at his mum who wipes her eyes.

"Darth is dead. We suspected as much, but this letter came back today from some survivors. We sent out two dragons to look for anyone that needed help, and they found a big group of all women and children who claim Darth saved them," Kor's mum explains, and I reach out, taking her hand.

"I will never forget Darth and how he saved Kor's life. He saved us all, and that is something I can never repay. I am so sorry your father has passed on," I say, feeling overwhelming sadness that such a brilliant man is now gone. Kor kisses the side of my head, wrapping an arm around me as his father comes over and takes his mother away.

"I'm sorry he is gone, Kor," I say, pressing my head into the side of his arm.

"Me too. I suspect he won't be the only one we say goodbye to before all of this is over." His words stay with me as we hold each other, each of us hoping he is wrong.

CHAPTER 18

ISOLA

I slowly watch as the two suns rise over the tree line as I sit on the roof of the academy, soaking in the peace of the moment. The suns cast yellow, orange and pink streaks across the sky like a vivid painting. The beauty, so lovely for a day that will bring so much death. It just reminds me that the suns will always rise, no matter how bad the night was. It's something you can always count on. The sunrises are the most peaceful and beautiful thing in every world. I should be training, learning something but I know unless I calm myself down, I won't be able to focus on what is needed to win this war.

"Hey, kitty cat. You sure pick an easy place to hide," Dagan mutters from behind me, and I turn to see him climbing up the roof with Eli, Thorne and Kor next to him. They all have dragon leather on, making them look even more handsome, and their cloaks fly around in the wind as they climb up.

Must make sure mine survive war, my dragon protectively purrs into my mind, and I agree with her in every sense as I stare at my dragons.

I will do everything I can to make sure they live. We will do everything we can, I explain to her.

We strong, she tells me.

Together, yes, we are, I tell my dragon as my guys get to me, feeling a strange sense of proudness from her. They all come and sit down next to me, Eli and Thorne sitting on my sides, whereas Dagan sits by Thorne and Kor sits next to Eli. I rest my head on Thorne's shoulder as she takes my hand in his, linking our fingers. We all happily watch the suns rise together, knowing this very well could be the last moment we all get alone together.

"Whatever happens today, I need you to know I love all of you with every little bit of my heart," I say, my voice catching in my throat as it feels like a ball of sadness is stuck there. I've never even admitted there might be a slight chance we won't make it out of this, and now I need to face that fact. An army of dead dragon guards is coming for us, and it will not be easy to escape this with all of us alive.

"We know, doll," Kor replies, and I look over at him. "Like I'm sure you know how much we adore you."

"I suspect you like me a little bit," I tease, making them all chuckle. "What do you imagine for us when this is all over?" I ask, wanting to know what they think. I've always imagined we will do up the castle and make it more homey for us before moving in. When this is over, I plan to send whatever is left of my dragon guard to the villages to help them rebuild their lives rather than protect me. Dragon guard is no more, so only those who want to be guards can be. There are no more curses on Dragca, and I want to be a queen my people choose to follow. The most important things are making sure my people are safe, have homes, and have food in their stomachs. I will spend the first month travelling around Dragca myself with my guys and healing the land with Bee. I want to see Dragca and really understand my world like I've never gotten a chance to do before.

"I don't know about the others, but I imagine ruling at your side as your equal, helping you set up a council for each village and place rules that benefit our people as well as keep them safe. I also want to wake up with you every morning and get you break-fast," Thorne says, and I agree with the first part completely, whereas the second bit makes me laugh.

"Before your run with me and a fly with our dragons to stretch their wings," Kor adds in, and I scrunch my face at him. I thought we dropped that running every morning thing.

"Then we could train together before we have dinner, and I want to help train a new army of dragon guards. Dragons who are not forced to fight but want to have the honour of protecting the royal family. We could make a future that every dragon in Dragca wants to be part of," Dagan carries on, and Eli finishes the idea.

"I believe in setting your sister up as the royal seer and making a law that recognises seers as people equal to dragons. They shouldn't be living in the woods when this is all over. I also think there should be classes in Dragca Academy, teaching young dragons and seers about light and dark magic. It shouldn't be hunted like it always has been." I nod at Elias's ideas and try not to cry at how he has clearly thought all this out for our future. "Before we sit around a fire every night, with you reading a new book and us watching those Earth movies we like."

"Will there be hot chocolate added into this plan?" I tease, wanting to know the important stuff.

"Of course, doll," Kor replies with a little chuckle.

"Do you think we will win tonight?" I quietly ask them, wanting to know what they think.

"I know that no matter what happens, we will always be with each other," Eli says, his words seem to drift in the wind, all of us not wanting to say a word. It's a long time before Dagan stands up, stretching his arms out.

"We should fly for a bit, all of us together. It will let our dragons have that time together," Dagan suggests, and I smile as I let him help me up. I walk to the edge of the roof and look over my shoulder at my dragons as they walk to me.

"Let's fly!" I shout over the wind before jumping off the roof, letting my dragon take over to fly with her mates.

CHAPTER 19

ISOLA

Turn right, Thorne directs in my mind, and I swing around with my spear, hitting the moving wooden target straight in the middle of its chest. I pull my spear out and quickly swing back and hit the one I sense a little to my left, right in the middle again. The targets all move around me until Thorne switches them off, and they stay still. This turned out to be the perfect distraction when I needed it more than I knew. I've been running around the academy, trying to help however I can and likely just getting in the way. Dagan and Thorne suggested some training might help.

"You've gotten better," Dagan states, smiling at me as I get my breath back in the cold room that smells like sweat and blood. Dagan only has on a thin white shirt with leather trousers, and it makes him look like a sexy pirate. I glance over at Thorne as he comes over, putting his bow down along with his arrows after pulling them out of his own targets. Thorne has a cloak on that hides his leather clothes. There is no one but Thorne, Dagan and me in here as not many people are using the guards' training rooms today since they are getting ready at the border for tonight. Even the thought that war is coming in only a few hours scares me more than I like.

"Here," Thorne offers me a bottle of water just as the doors open, and Winter walks in with her angel mate at her side. They are both dressed in leather, kitted out with deadly looking weapons, and seem serious, which worries me. We all walk over, as I smile at Winter.

"Have you come to train with me?" I ask her, curious about why she would clearly search for me. The last I checked, Winter was helping stock the basement where we are hiding all the people who cannot fight. She was also wrestling that little demon of hers down there as Milo wants to fight. I don't know how a tiny demon is going to fight a dragon, but I imagine it would be a sight to see.

"No, I wanted to talk to you about something important that I don't know how to ask," she says, looking nervous.

"Oh?" I ask, crossing my arms and wondering what she could want to speak to me about.

"Why don't you all leave Dragca and come back to Earth? We will destroy the portals, and no one could ever get through again. Tatarina will eventually die, and then maybe one day someone could go back," she suggests an idea I've thought more than once about. I love that she has asked, that she is trying to protect me. It just can't happen. There are a million reasons why not, like the fact Bee would struggle to live on Earth, but Dragca is my home. And there is one pressing issue I would never risk. It is a future I will fight for and never run away from.

"It would be best for your people. We can easily find somewhere safe for you to live," Dabriel kindly says, folding his arms as he and Winter wait for my reply.

"I can't," I reply, shaking my head.

"Why? This is dangerous here, and we might not win," Winter asks. "Coming to Earth might be running, but it would be safe for us all. I want what is best, but I fought for Earth and my people, so I will understand if you want to stay and fight."

"It's not just about my people, it's so much more than that. If I have a child in the future, I promised to bring her here. To your aunt, a fate. This neck-lace is my promise, so my child would pay the price of me running away. I won't run, though I do thank you for your offer. I know you are just trying to find a way to make sure I live through this," I explain to her, reaching out and taking her hand in mine before squeezing it tightly. She sighs with a sad look.

"It was worth a shot," she says, glancing at Dabriel. "We will leave you now to get our people ready. We can win this, because I am not losing my new friend."

"I hope so, because I want us to be friends for a long time," I say, and she hugs me tightly before walking off, Dabriel's arm wrapped around her shoulders. Dagan and Thorne watch her go for a while before either of them says anything.

"Come on, I want to show you guys something,"

Dagan says, reaching for my hand and linking our fingers. Thorne nods his head as I look back at him and let Dagan lead us out of the training room and down through two doors that look like they lead to a basement. Dagan switches a light on, illuminating a tunnel, as Thorne shuts the doors behind us.

"This is a good idea for a mini break," Thorne tells Dagan.

"I'm the smart one, you see," Dagan cheekily replies, and I laugh as I rest my head on his shoulder as he walks us down the corridor. The corridor opens up into a large room which has steam rising from the floor, making the room foggy. There are wooden benches all around for seating and even some towels folded by the entrance on a cabinet.

"It's the steam rooms, or sauna, as humans call it. After intense training, it is a good place to come and chill out," Dagan says, stepping back from me, and he starts pulling his clothes off. I glance back to see Thorne pushing his trousers down, and I admire the sight of my mates for a moment before I follow their lead. I used to get nervous undressing in front of anyone, but with them, my mates, it just seems natural. I'm surprised they are so okay with

G. BAILEY

being naked near each other though. I finish pulling my clothes off before going to sit down on the wooden seat, as I feel Thorne and Dagan sit on either side of me.

"Do you want children when you're older then?" Dagan suddenly asks, no doubt thinking about it from what I said to Winter.

"Yes. I want a child I can give a good life to. What about you two?" I ask both Dagan and Thorne, looking between them.

"I never thought about a future, a life with children or any of that, until I met you, Isola. You know I didn't have a good upbringing with my mother. I have no idea who my father is...I soon realised that the one thing I missed the most was being loved by my mother when she was gone. She didn't have money, neither could she really look after us, but she kept us fed and happy. I miss her laugh when I think of her. She had the sweetest laugh. I want my child to be loved, unconditionally. I predict we all can have that future, together," Dagan says, making my heart feel happy as I look at him for a moment. I never knew how he felt about children, but there is one thing for sure, any child of mine will have one mother and four dads to keep an eye on them. Love will be one thing that will never be missing.

Thorne adds, "I feel the same. I want a future with you and dozens of children running around, driving us crazy," and we laugh as he links his fingers with mine, pulling them up and kissing the back.

"Dozens?" I chuckle. "I was thinking more like one or two."

"Yeah, one or two is enough. We will never get time alone with Issy if we have more," Dagan says, laughing with Thorne as I rest my head on his shoulder. We all sit with each other for a long time, just content in being with each other and relaxing. I love this moment with them, my mates. Everything is going wrong, nothing is promised to us and it makes me just want to be close as possible to those I love before tonight. I move my hand to Dagan's thigh and slowly slide my hand up, finding his length hard and waiting for me.

"Kitty cat, you really do have a naughty streak," he groans as I reach my other hand for Thorne, wrapping my hand around him at the same time. I stroke them both, enjoying the way they buck their hips, and Thorne's hand goes to the back of my head, turning me to kiss him. Dagan moves my hand off him to kneel behind me, turning me on my side. His hand goes straight to my core, easily slipping one finger inside of me. I moan into Thorne's mouth as he gently grabs one of my breasts and starts rubbing my nipple. Dagan kisses my back as his finger thrusts in and out of me, my moans swallowed up by Thorne's mouth.

I move my lips away from Thorne's lips and kiss down his body until I find his length and take it deep in my mouth. Dagan mutters something I can't hear as he pulls his finger out and spreads my legs as he kneels behind me before sliding deep inside me. I cry out in pleasure around Thorne's length as he thrusts in and out of my mouth, his hand still teasing my nipple as his other hand is in my hair. The room is full of only the sounds of my moans and their grunts as we all chase our finish. Dagan reaches around and rolls his thumb in a circle around my clit, as he thrusts in and out of me. Only seconds later, I come, feeling Dagan coming deep inside me a few thrusts later, and Thorne pulls me off him, sliding me onto his hips and thrusting deep. I lock eyes with his silver ones as his dragon roars while I roll my hips, and he groans, finishing with a loud roar that shakes the room. I collapse onto his chest, breathless and completely satiated as I glance at Dagan who is catching his breath with a grin on his lips.

"This is the perfect way to prepare for war," he says, and I laugh, holding Thorne closer as I know this could be the last moments we all have together.

CHAPTER 20

ISOLA

The wind whips my braid and cloak to the side as I stand at the edge of the forest with my dragons at my side, watching the tree line for any movement. My heart pounds in my chest as I smell the fire and scent of death in the wind. Whatever is coming our way is not going to be easy to win or beat. I only have to find Nane and Tatarina though—and pray my army with Winter's can beat whoever Tatarina is sending our way. Winter stands close with her mates, all of us just in the boundary of Dragca Academy as we wait for the army that is heading our way. I want to be here for when Tatarina gets to me as I have no clue how she plans to break the ancient spell that prevents anyone meaning ill harm to the academy from being on the land. Bee places her hand on my cheek, and I give her a worried glance.

"You should be back in the castle where it is safe," I whisper to her, and she shakes her head, moving her green hair around. I glance at my mates, catching each of their eyes and feeling their worry in our bond. They are worried about me, and as I turn my head to Eli, I know he is feeling the same. I want to tell them it is all going to be alright, but that would be a lie, and I know it.

"No. End is here, and I am with you. You are the balance," she whispers to me just as I sense something coming our way, and I have to give up my argument with Bee. I press my stone on my staff, and it slides out in my hand as everyone gets their weapons out at the same time. I watch the trees as a single dragon guard walks out, his feet dragging across the ground with every step. His skin is grey, though his eyes are black with black lines crawling down his face that almost seem to move. He stops a few inches away from us. In a seriously creepy way, he tilts his head to the side, his movements seem like a puppet, and we all know who is pulling the strings.

"I h-have a message from the true qu-queen," he

grumbles out, his words about understandable to me. "The army will fight here, but she waits for Isola in the castle. Come to her, and the war can be stopped. The war ends in the castle, not in the academy." After his actually well spoken words, he holds a shaky arm up in the air, and dozens of dragon guards run at us as he stands still. I look up as countless dragons with dry black skin slam into the barrier at the same time the soldiers do. It burns them, but the more they push, the more the invisible barrier gets closer to us.

"It can't hold them, we need to get ready," Dagan states, dropping his swords and stepping back, his eyes drifting across the soldiers blasting the barrier, causing little cracks. The dragons above start blasting fire against it, and I know that the moment it breaks, it's going to be hell. There are so many of them here, surrounding us almost. I glance back at our army, seeing how so many of their faces look scared.

"Shift with me, and we will fight in the sky for our queen! For Dragca!" Dagan shouts, and there are loud war cries as people shout for Dragca before shifting, their dragons letting out loud roars as they fly up in the sky. Winter and her mates start barking orders to their men, many of them shifting into wolves, and angels start flying into the sky underneath where the dragons fly around. Dagan comes to me and harshly kisses me, making my lips prickle, before stepping back, and I don't want to let him go. I know he needs to though. Our people need him more than me right now. Dagan isn't my dragon guard anymore, he is now guarding all of our people like my other mates. Like Eli.

"You don't go to her, you hear me? She wants you dead," Dagan firmly warns me, but I don't reply before he steps back and starts running. He shifts quickly, turning into his huge dragon and taking to the sky as I look back at Thorne, Kor and Eli at my sides. Melody and Hallie step closer, as do Winter and the giant wolf at her side. Her other mates are with their army, getting them ready.

"Any moment now," I warn, holding my staff up and locking eyes with Thorne.

"We do this, and then we get my mother. It has to be done," Thorne says, and I see the pain in his eyes he tries to hide from me. I feel it through our bond. He knows she has to die today, but she is still his mother. I don't want him there when I do this. It would hurt him even more to see her die.

"I know," I reply, moving my eyes back to the line of soldiers just as there is a bright white light and a whoosh of air hits me directly in the stomach as the barrier breaks, sending me flying backwards into my army behind me. I try to roll as I land, managing to only stop myself after a few spins. I cough and pull myself up to my feet, seeing that we have all been thrown in different directions. I pick Bee up off the floor, seeing a lump on her head where she was hurt from the blast. I can feel her heartbeat under my hand.

I hear footsteps behind me and turn, holding a hand out and blasting shards of ice at the three dead dragon guards that were running for me. They fall to the floor, smashing into black and red dust. I frantically look around as I stand up, not seeing anyone I recognise as I sense my mates are alive and somewhere near. I look up as Dagan and my army of dragons fight Tatarina's dead army. The fight is all claws, blood, fire and pain as they rip each other apart, moving so quickly that I can't see who is winning.

"Give her to me," Winter suggests, getting to my side just as two of the dead dragon guard get to us. I hand Bee over and quickly hold my hands out, freezing the two guards dead on the spot and kicking them over as they smash into dust before looking back. Winter has a little bag on her back which she tucks Bee into before nodding at me.

"Time to fight," she says, unclipping a dagger, and I turn to look around for my dragons, not seeing them anywhere. I do see a bunch of at least twenty dragon guards attacking my people, and I decide to help them. I lift my spear up and pull back, waiting for the perfect moment as I run and fling it into two of the guards. They scream, burning up where the spear touches them as I slam three shards of ice into more guards.

I watch in amazement as I run, seeing Winter shooting beams of blue energy into more guards, and they turn into dust. She also somehow throws daggers at them as she runs with me. *Damn, she is cool.* When I get to the burnt guards, I pick up my spear and slam it into a dragon guard bent over a woman who is screaming. He explodes into red dust, covering all of me as I cough and kneel down to see the woman, who is in a bad way. I wipe my eyes to see her better, her long red hair mixes in with the blood pouring out from a hole in her neck. She coughs out blood as I hold her hand, knowing she won't have long now before death takes her.

"My queen," she splutters, grabbing my hand tightly.

"I'm here. I'm sorry," I whisper, trying to stay strong for her in her last moments even though I wish I could have saved her, but her body is covered in stab wounds, and I feel powerless in this moment.

"Finish the war," she pleads before her head rolls to the side, and I realise I don't even know the name of the dragon who just died for me. I close her eyes with my fingers, leaving trails of red dust over them before I stand up. I look around at the war around me, seeing nothing but pain, blood and death in every direction. There is so much darkness, so much destruction, and Tatarina caused it all. *She must pay.*

I spot Hallie and Melody across the field just as Winter kills two more dragon guards near me then comes to my side. She looks down at the woman's body sadly before pulling her eyes to me, waiting for a plan.

"This way," I say, knowing I need to get to my sister first and then my mates. We run across the field, and I shoot shards of ice at anyone that gets close.

We head for my sister and Hallie who are fighting off at least eight dragon guards on their own, jumping over dead bodies and piles of dust on the ground that I know will be stuck in my memory for a long time. One of the dragon guards gets too close and hits Melody on the head, knocking her to the ground before he lifts his sword for the final blow.

"NO!" I scream, running as fast as I can, knowing I am too far away to stop this. Hallie quickly jumps in front of Melody as the sword comes down, and I scream.

CHAPTER 21

ISOLA

*W*inter and I blast blue energy and ice at the remaining dead guards as we get to my sister and Hallie on the floor. Melody is holding Hallie in her arms, crying as she rocks her and strokes her face. There is so much blood on all of them. I fall next to her, touching Melody's shoulder as I look down at the massive sword cut all across Hallie's chest. She is crying out in pain but alive at least. A sob escapes my lips as my shaky hand touches her cheek.

"Can you call Dabriel? Can he heal her?" I turn to ask Winter, and she nods, wiping a tear away as she mentally calls her mate. The giant wolf gets to her side, along with Atticus and a bunch of my dragons who circle us, protecting us against the dead guards for a moment.

"I love you. You can't die, this can't happen. It was meant to be me," Melody pleads through her tears as I take Hallie's cold hand into mine and squeeze it tight as she cries. Hallie opens her eyes, staring at Melody and no doubt talking to her in her mind. I look around, hearing more screams, seeing fire blast across the sky as another dragon falls out of the clouds. There is so much pain, and if I don't stop Tatarina, it won't stop.

"I have to go. I have to finish this," I tell them both, and Melody shakes her head, grabbing my wrist as I try to stand.

"No, I have to come with you or—" she starts off as I take her hand off me.

"You've warned me. Stay with your mate, I have to do this," I shakily say. I stand up and step back before looking up at the dozens of dragons fighting in the sky above me. It's going to be difficult to fly out here, but if anybody can do it, my dragon and I can.

"Winter, please give me Bee," I walk over and ask her. She nods, pulling me to the side a little as more of my army protect us, fighting for us. I know Melody and Hallie will be safe.

"Dabriel is far away. He is trying to get here, but it might not be quick enough to save her," she warns me, offering me the bag off her shoulder. I grab the strap tightly as I take one more look at my best friend and sister, wishing that I could help them in some way. I can't save Hallie and go after Tatarina though.

"Protect them for me as I have to go to stop this war," I manage to say. Winter agrees as I grab my spear and walk back a little before shifting into my dragon form. I knock a few dead dragon guards out of the way as I fly into the air, holding Bee in the bag in my claws. My dragon flies low towards the trees, just as I hear my mates argue with me in my mind, wanting me to come back.

Isola, don't you dare go alone. Wait for us, they plead as I spot two familiar looking dragons flying over to me, closely following me. It's Eli and my uncle, I think. I know Eli won't go back now, and I can't make him. I didn't want him there when I faced Tatarina. *Dammit.*

I need Nane, but I love each one of you. Always, I reply

and block them out before they can say another word as they need to focus on the fight as well. Eli and my uncle get to my side, flying close as the dragon guards just let us go. She wants me to come to her. I roar as I speed up to the castle, flying as quickly as I can past the dead trees surrounding it.

There is danger. We should leave, my dragon hisses to me, and I sense her fear.

If we leave, there will be nothing but danger and death that will never stop following us. We can do this together, I tell her, and she lets out a loud, confident roar that helps me feel a little better as we get to the castle. It looks worse than the last time we were here, more dead plants climb the walls, and yet there is nobody around this time as we all land after I carefully put Bee down in the bag. I shift back and quickly pull my spear out as Eli and my uncle shift back as well. Bee climbs out the bag, seeming a little paler green than I'm used to seeing her looking, but she is okay.

"Nane is near," Bee tells me, her wide eyes glancing towards the door.

"I know. We are going to save her," I say, patting my shoulder, and she lands on it as my uncle and Eli come to me.

"You shouldn't be here. Tatarina could get control of you again," I hiss at Eli, who just looks at me with a stubborn face.

"She can't control me anymore. I won't leave you alone, so forget it. Now what is the plan?" Eli asks, dismissing my worry. I grit my teeth in frustration, knowing I won't be able to convince him to just leave me here. *It won't matter if I can get Nane.*

"I need to get Nane alone, just for a bit. Can you distract Tatarina?" I ask them and my uncle nods, rubbing his beard.

"We can, but you won't have long. They will be together, and she is expecting you," he warns me, picking up a sword off the ground he must have carried here. Eli has one too.

"I know it isn't going to be easy, but she can't die until I've bonded with Nane," I warn them. "Understood?" They both nod in agreement, but I have a feeling they won't listen if they get a chance to kill her. I walk forward, keeping my spear at my side ready as we go through the main doors to the castle which are left open. The inside is a ruin of cracked stone, dead plants and blood on the floor. The wallpaper is ripped, the old paintings lay in ruins on the floor. The beauty of my old home is gone, left in a mess of what remains. I walk across the cold stone to the throne room, knowing this is where it will all end. It's what this war is all about after all.

Tatarina sits on the throne, her eyes drifting to me in an almost unnatural way as she suddenly smiles when I stop in the middle of the room. Tatarina looks worse than ever before, more touched by a darkness she could never control. Her once blonde hair is black, looking dry and horrible as it sticks around her shoulders. Her eyes are black like the lines crawling down her pale cheeks. She is emaciated, her blue dress barely held up on her body. Nane sits on her hand, though she only looks at Bee and not anyone else.

"Oh Tatarina, what has dark magic done to you?" I question, tilting my head to really look at her and how much she is a sorry state of herself.

"Nothing that doesn't make me better than I already am," she purrs, her voice deep and cracking like a witch.

"This is not better. *You are wrong.* Nane was never meant to be yours, she was meant to be mine," I say, and Nane lifts her head at the sound of her name.

"NO! You will not steal my power and my throne after you have already stolen my son!" Tatarina spits out, standing up as Nane flies near her, her eyes focused on Bee once again. I don't dare look at Bee as I want to make sure Tatarina stays in my sight.

"Have you even seen what you look like these days?" my uncle asks, stepping closer. "Isola didn't steal Thorne from you, you gave him up to get your dream. Is it all worth it? Are you truly happy as you sit alone in here?

"You look like death, which you will be familiar with soon enough," she says, though from her tone alone, I can tell she is getting more annoyed as I step to the side, heading for Nane as my uncle raises his sword, walking up to her.

"It is not me that is going to die. I will live with family and find myself a new life. You will die alone, with no one to mourn you. Not even your son," my uncle replies, filling my heart with hope as I take another step towards Nane who starts flying towards me. Well, not me, Bee.

"Oh Elias, how I have missed my slave. One touch

and you will be back in the darkness that you belong in," Tatarina purrs.

"No fucking way in hell. I'd rather die," Eli replies, just as Nane shoots a blast of dark magic straight at us, sending me flying across the room, but luckily, I catch Bee before I slam against the wall. Looking up, I see Eli go flying in the air from a wave of magic, and Tatarina grabs my uncle by his neck, lifting him off the ground. I scream as she stabs a dagger through my uncle's heart, and he lets out a scream that will forever haunt me, then she throws him across the room like a toy. Tatarina locks her eyes with mine before she begins to talk as she slowly walks over.

"Now the pawns are out of the way, isn't it time for the queens to play?"

CHAPTER 22

THORNE

I jump in the air, pulling out another arrow before I shoot it into the chest of a dead guard who was running at me, then turn around and look for the others as the dead guard explodes into dust. There are dragons dying, screams and so much pain around me, making it difficult to focus on anyone through it all. I spot Korbin on his own, fighting a big bunch of dead guards and run as fast as I can to him. I pass Essna with a few seers, who are making quick work of killing off the dead guards with their powers, though I know they won't be able to do that forever. Every part of me wants to shift into my dragon and fly to the castle to help Isola, but I know Dagan is doing that. Eli and her uncle are with her, and that has to be enough to give her a chance to win this once and for all. Even if it means killing my mother. A deep part of me knows I am mourning the idea of a mother rather than the person my mother actually is. I said goodbye to her a long time ago, and it's about time I accepted that. I will remember my adoptive parents because they were really who brought me up in the end.

I let out a long whistle when I get close enough, drawing a good load of the dead guards my way as I pull out some daggers. I get two of them in their chests before going to grab my bow when arms wrap around me from behind, pulling meto the ground as I fight them off. I slide a dagger out from my thigh as the dead guard bites down on my shoulder. *Fucking hell that hurt.* I slam my dagger into his stomach, making him let me go just as two dead guards run at me with long swords headed my way. I hold up a wall of flames with my hands, burning them to pieces that fall all over me before I stand up, coughing on the ash. My eyes widen as I hear a noise, looking up to see a dragon falling out of the sky and directly for me. I run and jump over a body, just getting out the way as it lands with a thump. I look around as Kor finishes off the dead guards around him and runs over to me. We stand back to back as we fight more of the dead guards coming at us, and I frown as I see an angel falling from the sky. Isn't that Winter's mate?

"Kor, that way!" I shout, pointing an arm at the angel just as he lands on the ground, sending dust and ash flying everywhere. We fight our way over to the angel, standing over him until Kor gives me a nod to check the angel as he fights the remaining dead guards. I lean down, seeing the burns on his arms that don't look good, but I suspect the cut on his head is why he fell. I nearly jump as Atticus appears out of nowhere right next to us and falls to Dabriel's side. Atticus is covered in blood, his clothes ripped, and he doesn't look in a good state. I guess fighting dragons wasn't so easy. I look around us, seeing that there aren't many of our army left standing here, and there is a massive load of dead guards running our way. The academy steps lay right behind us, and if they pass us, then the people hiding in there will have no one to protect them. That isn't happening. The witch and angel both need to get out of here.

"Wake up, you moody sod!" he shakes Dabriel's

shoulder, and Dabriel groans, coughing out dust as we both help him sit up. Kor lights up a ring of fire around us, temporarily defending us for a moment as we take a breather.

"Winter needs me," Dabriel suddenly says, still coughing as he looks at his burnt arms. Atticus lifts him up to stand up before making water appear in his hands and washing Dabriel's arms even though he screams out in pain from it. "Thank you, brother," Dabriel says, and I see that bond between them like I have with Dagan, Kor and even Elias now. We might not be brothers by blood, but that doesn't matter one bit. We are family, all in love with one fantastic woman who we will defend with our lives.

"Grab my arm, dragons, you should come with us. It's dangerous here," Atticus suggests as Kor and I lock eyes before turning away from the witch to face the hundred or more dead guards running at us. We don't have to talk through the bond to understand each other and what we know we have to do.

"Go! We have this. We will hold the academy doors," I tell Atticus, who bows his head before disappearing. The circle of fire disappears around us just as the army get close, and I lift my sword.

"For Isola," I say to Kor, who bows his head, lifting his own sword.

"For our Isola."

CHAPTER 23

ISOLA

I crawl to my feet with a groan, feeling my ribs broken from the blast, and it's like all the oxygen has left my lungs with it. I cough a few times as I pick up my spear, seeing an angry Bee fly out of my hands and straight towards Nane, blasting her with a ball of light. Nane fights back, both of them hurting each other, and I know I need to stop it. Light and dark blasts against each other, neither of them winning but both of them struggling as the power darkens the room, making all the fires go out.

"You are no queen, Tatarina," I turn to her, knowing I only have to hurt her enough to hold her down, and then I can get Nane and save Eli before killing Tatarina. The plan will still work. I swallow the pain as I lock eyes with Tatarina, not seeing any part of Thorne in her anymore. I thought it might hurt to kill his mother, but at this point, it is all I want and hope he will forgive me eventually. *She has to die.*

"And you think you are one? The silly little princess lost on Earth with no parents. Well you had a daddy, but he was too busy with me to bother with you. Does it hurt that he chose me? That he never wanted you all those years ago?" she laughs, holding her hands out and sliding out two daggers that must have been hidden on her wrists.

"My father was a monster, and you two belonged together. I had a good life on Earth. One I would never change for anything," I reply to her, and her face contorts in frustration. We circle each other, hearing Nane and Bee fighting behind us. My uncle is dying by the throne, and I can't see where Eli is. She flings herself at me, and I duck, slinging my spear across her leg as I go, and she cries out in pain. I spin around just as she throws one of her daggers at me, scratching my cheek, and I gasp. She limps to the left, spinning her dagger around before making a sword of pure ice in her other hand.

"Nice trick," I say, and she laughs as I copy her, making myself a second spear. We run at each other at the same time, her sword blasting into my spear as she tries to stab me with the dagger, but I use my other spear to knock it out of her hands before I push her back. She falls over, and I walk to her as she picks herself up. My eyes widen in horror as Eli appears behind Tatarina, holding a sword to her neck.

"Don't kill her! You can't," I cry out, stepping closer with every word to see if I can stop him. If he kills her, he will die because I won't be able to bond to Nane in time to save him. Elias looks over at me with so much love in his eyes, and it breaks my heart because I know what he is going to do. Melody's warning enters my mind, the one where she told me to duck as I try to figure out a way to save Eli.

"I'd do anything to save you. *Anything.* Including this," he says, lifting his sword to make the final blow as I run towards them both, screaming in pure terror of losing Eli. Tatarina shoots a bolt of ice right towards me, and I fall to the ground, the ice bolt cutting the top of my shoulder. If I hadn't ducked, that would have gone through my heart and killed me. I look up as Eli slams the sword down over Tatarina's neck, cutting her head off, and her blood splatters all over him as her head rolls across the floor. I cry out, not for Tatarina, but for Eli as he drops the sword and screams in pain.

"I'm not going to let the darkness take you. Never," I whisper, pulling myself off the floor and standing up. "You once told me our love was impossible, but it is not. I will save you."

"Let me go!" Elias shouts, shaking his head as he cries out in pain, black lines crawling all over his face. I see Bee and Nane floating around each other just behind me, trying to kill each other, and yet they are equal. They are sisters, and they can't do it. I know what has to happen. *No matter the cost.*

"Nane, you were never meant for Tatarina…You were mine from the start. You appeared for me when I was only a baby in my mother's womb. Tatarina found you instead," I say, knowing with every part of my soul that I am right.

"Run!" Elias pleads, and tears stream down my face as I take another step forward, right into the middle of Nane and Bee. They both fly at me, and I hold both my arms out, keeping my eyes locked with Elias as he realises what I'm about to do.

"No, they will kill you!" he shouts, just as Nane and Bee touch my hands, and pain ripples through every part of my body. The dark and light attack me at the same time, making me feel like I'm being ripped apart. The pain is indescribable, and for a moment, I can only cry out in agony.

"Stop," I cry out, and the pain slows, only for what feels like a second, and I can open my eyes. My body is floating, there is a half white and black orb of smoke surrounding me, and I can't see the room anymore.

"Light or dark, there must be a choice," Nane demands, and I turn to her, seeing only a scared spirit who doesn't know who she is. Or who she belongs to.

"I think you will find I'm good at sharing. I will share with you both and love you both equally. You are mine, both light and dark. I am your balance, and I'm so sorry you didn't have me at your side until now. We were meant to be all together, to bring peace to Dragca. To save it," I say, and tears stream down her face as she walks up my arm before sitting on my shoulder.

"Save, no more fighting," she says quietly, her little voice filled with pain. "Darkness no more if that is what you want."

"The world needs the dark, or you would never see the light," Bee comments as she sits on my other shoulder. I smile proudly at her, knowing she is right. I don't want to get rid of the darkness, I just want to cause a balance.

"Let's save Dragca and my Eli. We need balance, and we must drain the darkness that is killing Dragca," I say, watching Nane's reaction because it is important she agrees. She nods, and I float down to the floor. I place my hands on the cracked ground and look up, seeing Elias's body lying on the floor near me, knowing he will never survive if I don't do this. I must drain the darkness out of him as well, pull it back to me, and keep him bonded to me forever.

"For Dragca," I whisper and close my eyes, slamming my power into the ground and pulling all the darkness I can find until everything disappears, and I feel myself falling with no chance of saving myself.

CHAPTER 24

ISOLA

TWO MONTHS LATER.

"*L*ink to the heart, link to the soul. I pledge my heart to you, for you, for all the time I have left. My dragon is yours, my love is yours, and everything I am, belongs with you," I say to Eli, not able to keep the huge grin off my face as our mating stone glows brightly in the priest's hands. We both let the priest cut our hands before placing them together, and the stone glows so brightly I can only see Eli in the room as the priest speaks. *My Eli*. I still relive the moment when I bonded with Nane and Bee; I managed to push enough light and dark into what was left of my Eli and save him. We are bonded in a strange way now, one that means we can sense each other, and I can keep him alive as long as I live. Eli has grown out his black hair, so it is similar to how we met, and his suit fits him lovely, showing off his muscles from the training he has been doing with Dagan and the new dragon guard army.

"Light and dark, good and evil, and everything that makes us dragons, please bless this mating. We bless you," the priest says, and the light blasts brightly as Eli pulls me into his arms and spins me around, making me laugh before he kisses me.

"We bless you," the hundreds of people in the throne room cheer as Eli puts me down and then turns to the priest. He picks up one of the four king crowns on the side as I walk past my other mates to stand in front of my father's throne. There are four new thrones, two on each side of me now, one for each of the kings of Dragca. I glance over at my uncle on the front row of my guests, holding hands with Essna. I was lucky Bee managed to save him from Tatarina's attack, and I was more surprised to find out he and Essna were in love. They mated a month ago while the castle was still being repaired, and now they run Dragca

Academy which is being rebuilt, made better for our new generations.

I move my eyes from them to Melody and Hallie, who are talking quietly to Jonas who they adopted. I brought Jonas back here with Jules, who sits next to Hallie's side and proudly smiles at me. A few other dragons' children came back from Winter's castle with new families found here, but others decided to stay. It's a good way to keep Jonas in the family as I want to make sure he has a good life. Melody and Hallie can give him that, and they make a cute little family. Dagan, Korbin and Thorne all kneel next to Eli, all of their heads bowed in respect.

"Do you accept the throne? To be kings of Dragca and always defend your queen?" the priest asks my mates, the words feeling so important as this is a massive change for Dragca. We have set up a new council, healed the villages, and with Winter's witches' help, it was easy to rebuild the destroyed homes. The last two months have gone so quickly, and this day has been anxiously anticipated. This is the first day of peace in Dragca, one that I hope will stretch on for generations.

They all have ruby red cloaks on that match my red dress, and their crowns have a mix of red and blue stones. It suits them, and they do very much look like kings of Dragca in this moment. I never would have expected this for our future, but I know it is perfect.

"For our entire lives, I will, and I accept," they all say in union. I watch as the priest places a crown on each of their heads before moving back.

"Then rise, kings of Dragca," the priest says. As my kings rise up, the priest disappears into white dust. My kings come and stand in front of their thrones at my side, and we all sit down at the same time. Every dragon, seer and supernatural in the throne room cheers as I send a message to my mates.

I love you all.

*T*run a comb through my daughter's hair as she sits on a stool smiling at me in the reflection of the mirror in front of us. My daughter is a mini-me, her long blonde hair is the same colour as mine, and she has my blue eyes. Though I don't know who her father is exactly, it has never mattered. She calls them all dad. The day she was born, the whole of Dragca cheered and celebrated the royal birth. The pregnancy was long and difficult, and Jules was with me the whole time. Jules loves Dragca and my daughter, and I hope we still have many years with her yet.

Melody and Hallie adopted a baby girl only a year ago, a seer whose mother passed away. Jonas loves his new sister, and they live happily in the castle with us now. Every day, Jonas looks more like his brother, only his eyes are a little different. It makes me happy because I know Jace isn't all gone from the worlds. He is here with us.

"I can't believe you are five today, Emery. My baby is getting all grown up," I say, braiding her hair as she giggles at me. I slide her silver tiara on her head, before sliding some clips into hold it into place.

"Mummy, I'm a little girl now. Not a baby anymore," she tells me, and I can't help but laugh at her sassy answer. I swear my child is more sarcastic than anyone in the whole of Dragca.

"Oh, I'm sorry, miss little girl. I didn't realise. How foolish of me," I reply, enjoying her laugh. I finish her hair, and she slides off the seat. "Do little girls still hold their mummy's hand as we go to their birthday parties?"

"Of course, mummy," she says, taking my hand as I smile down at her. It seems like only yesterday that she was born, and yet I have to accept she is growing up now. The price all parents deal with, I imagine. We walk out of her very pink bedroom, which is next door to our own rooms and down the corridor. I hear the children laughing before we even get to the ballroom, and two guards open the doors for us, bowing their heads. Emery lets go of my hand and runs into the room to Dagan, who catches her and swings her around as she giggles. He hugs her tightly before he puts her down and gives her a little present box from his jacket as I walk over. I see Jonas eating the food, Melody and Hallie are laughing with my uncle and Essna by the piano which Jules is playing a sweet song on. All the other children run over to see what the present is. I look back as Thorne places his hand on my back, kissing my cheek as we watch Emery rip the gift open and pull out a yellow collar.

"A collar? I don't understand," she says, seeming as confused as I am. I only know Dagan and Thorne left to go to Earth yesterday to get the present, and it is a big surprise. From the mischievous look Winter gave me when she got here yesterday, I know she had something to do with whatever this gift is.

"Well, you know how you really wanted a puppy from Earth? The ones like the stories mummy has told you?" Dagan asks, and he stands up, waving a hand at Elias and Korbin as they walk over with a black, fluffy, little puppy in their arms. The puppy is huge compared to puppies I've seen before, with pointy ears and glowing purple eyes, which looks like no Earth puppy I've ever seen before. It has been a year or so since I went anywhere but Winter's castle on Earth, but still, not that much has changed. Emery squeals and runs over, repeating thank you a million times as they give her the puppy to hold, and it licks her face with a purple tongue.

"A puppy in a dragon castle?" I question Thorne with a long sigh, and he laughs.

"It's not just a normal puppy. It's a little different, so don't worry," he replies. "Adelaide promised it will grow wings soon."

"Wait, wings? It's from Frayan? The crazy fairy place? And what do you mean 'different'? Not dangerous 'different', I hope," I rapid question him and look back over at Emery who is clearly in love with her new friend. I suppose she could freeze the flying puppy if it is dangerous.

"Nope, not dangerous," Thorne says with a big smirk at my over protective nature and kisses me before letting go. "I'm going to check out the food. Want to come?"

"No, thanks. I'm going to say hello to Winter," I say, nodding at my friend who is sitting heavily pregnant on a chair by the window. Thorne smiles at me before I walk over, pulling up a chair and sitting down to rest my sore feet.

"Being pregnant sucks, doesn't it?" Winter protests, and I look down at my little bump, knowing I have a while to go yet.

"Yes, but at least the morning sickness is gone for now," I admit. I always thought that was the worst of the start of pregnancy issues.

"Though I will admit this pregnancy is much easier than the twins were," Winter says, and I follow her gaze over to her children who are a year older than Emery, and they are all extremely close. We all joke that Lucian is Emery's shadow, and we hope they date one day, linking our families. Lucian and Emery tell us we are all embarrassing them, which always makes us laugh as they have bright red cheeks when they tell us off. Alina and Emery are very close too, like sisters really, and hate when they can't spend the weekends with each other.

The supernatural school is opening next month in Dragca, mirroring the one open on Earth already.

We have worked out a way to connect a portals between worlds that is in the schools, and Melody is starting a new class on all supernatural races. Bee and Nane helped with that. They have transformed the royal gardens into their homes, and it is more beautiful than it is ever has been there now. They actually get along pretty well now, and after everyone got used to the fact Nane isn't all bad, it got better. Shaking myself out of my daydreams, I watch my daughter playing with her new puppy, all her friends around her, and how loved and happy she is. My mates are laughing with Winter's mates, and they have become good friends since the war.

"I think I'm carrying twins. Well, at least that is what Bee and Nane tell me," I quietly say, because I haven't told my mates what Melody told me this morning. She said she had a vison of the future and all our children together. They are going to be rulers to be proud of.

"At least you have a few mates to help with two newborns, Isola," she says, and we both laugh. "It's hard work, but worth it. Everything has been worth it."

"Do you think we will always have peace now?" I ask her, and she looks towards me.

"The fates gave us this life as a reward, and we will have peace. We fought our battles, and I'm glad we survived," she tells me, reaching over and holding my hand. I rest my head back on the chair as Emery waves at me before running to Eli, and he picks her up, making her laugh with whatever he said to her. I rest my other hand on my bump, feeling my babies kick, and smile.

We did more than survive, we won our wars, and we now live a life that could never be forgotten. We thrived and fulfilled our destiny. We lived through our fate.

The end.

AUTHOR NOTE

Hello, and thank you for reading the Protected by Dragons series. I am still so shocked this series is over, but we will see Isola and her men in Adelaide's Trust. (Out next year).
Thank you to everyone that helped make this series possible. Like Mads, Helayna, Christian, Cora, the Cat's Pajamas and my amazing Pack Leaders.
Most of all, thank you to my readers.
You inspire me to keep writing every day.
With your kind reviews and amazing comments.
G.

Please keep reading for an excerpt from The Deadly Game...

Stalker Manual

Instagram
Facebook
Twitter
Pinterest

Join Bailey's Pack

Join <u>Bailey's Pack</u> on Facebook to stay in touch with the author, find out what is coming out next and any news!

WWW.GBAILEYAUTHOR.COM

G. Bailey's Book List

Her Guardians Series (Complete)-
Winter's Guardian (Book one)
Winter's Kiss (Book Two)
Winter's Promise (Book Three)
Winter's War (Book Four)

Her Fate Series-
(Her Guardians Series spinoff)
Adelaide's Fate (Book one)
Adelaide's Trust (Coming soon)

Saved by Pirates Series (Complete)-
Escape the sea (Book One)
Love the sea (Book Two)
Save the Sea (Book Three)
Saved by Pirates Collection with bonus content.
Lost Heir (Stand-alone based on Everly coming out soon)

One Night series-
Strip for Me- (Book one)

The Marked Series (Co-written with Cece Rose)-
Marked by Power- (Book One)
Marked by Pain- (Book Two)
Marked by Destruction- (Book Three)

G. Bailey's Book List

The Forest Pack series-
Run Little Wolf- (Book One)
Run Little Bear- (Book Two)
Run Little Prince (Coming out soon)
Run Little Beauty (Coming out soon)

Protected by Dragons series
(Complete and in the same world as Her Guardians/Her
Fate series)-
Wings of Ice-(Book One)
Wings of Fire- (Book Two)
Wings of Spirit- (Book Three)
Wings of Fate- (Book Four)
Wings of Dragca- (Coming November)

From the Stars-
True Light- (Book One)
Dark Soul- (Book Two)
Shadow Kiss (Coming soon)

A Demon's Fall series-
Runes of Truth- (Book One)
Runes of Mortality- (Book Two)
Runes of Black Magic- (Book Three)
Runes of Royalty- (Coming December)

G. Bailey's Book List

The King Brothers Series-
Secret (Book One)
Chance (Book Two)
Past (Book Three
Fall (Book Four)
Revenge (Coming out in November/December)

The Deadly Game
(Stand-alone co-wrote with CoraLee June)

The Familiar Empire-
The Missing Wolf (In the Petting Them Anthology)
The Found Wolf (Coming soon)

Dark Tales Series-
Tales & Time (In the Once Upon a Rebel Fairytale anthology)
Tales & Dreams (Coming soon)

The Forsaken Gods Trilogy
(Co-wrote with CoraLee June)-
Eternal Soul (Coming out in December)

Her Guardians official colouring book.

ABOUT THE AUTHOR

G. Bailey is a USA Today bestselling author of books that are filled with everything from dragons to pirates. Plus, fantasy worlds and breath-taking adventures. Oh, and some swoon-worthy men that no girl could forget. G. Bailey is from the very rainy U.K. where she lives with her husband, two children and three cheeky dogs. And, of course, the characters in her head that never really leave her, even as she writes them down for the world to read!

Please feel free say hello on here or head over to Facebook to join G. Bailey's group, Bailey's Pack! (Where you can find exclusive teasers, random giveaways and sneak peeks of new books on the way!)

Don't go outside.
Stay away from your windows. Don't look the witches in the eye.

Once a year, the bridge between the living and the dead is opened and witches compete in The Deadly Games for a chance to speak with those that have crossed over. Each coven needs a human to participate, and this year I'm forced to help the Hex Coven, a group of sexy witches mourning the loss of their brother. They're determined to find his killer, curses and evil covens be damned.

Humans rarely survive the games, and I've accepted that I won't make it to morning. Deciding to live this night like it's my last, I enjoy all the pleasures that the Hex Coven has to offer.

Because to speak to the dead, first you must die.

THE DEADLY GAME

It was unseasonably cool for this time of year. The leaves outside covered the ground, brushing against my boots with every step, as I walked back to my house on Main Street. Pumpkins sat rotting on my neighbor's porch and the smell of incense filled the air. I looked down at my phone, checking the alert flashing on the rectangular screen.

Curfew at 6:00PM. All humans not in their home at that time are forced to participate in the Deadly Games.

It was foolish of me to be out so close to the Deadly Games, but I'd just picked a fresh bouquet of flowers for Mama's grave, and I wanted to decorate her tombstone for Día de los Muertos. The witches might be the only ones able to communicate with the dead, but I still held hope that she'd see them and follow the trail of marigolds through our little town to my ofrenda. There was only one night a year that bridged the gap between the living and the afterlife, and after almost a year without her, I craved something—anything—that brought her memory alive.

I brushed my long, brown hair behind my ears and looked around, clutching my red jacket closer to my body. I was wearing long jeans and a button up shirt, but it did nothing to fight the chill. The street was deserted. Not many risked being outside just before the curfew—not unless they were one of the witch worshipers, those that *wanted* to play. Ever since I was a little girl, I'd been warned about the Deadly Games. My papa would tell me, *"Don't stand too close to the window. The witches will get you, Camila."*

One night a year, all the witches crossed the human border and came to our town to compete for a chance to talk to the dead. We shared a cemetery that was a magical hot spot of activity, necessary to win. I'd heard rumors about their deadly games.

The humans that participated were cursed.

They needed humans to complete each task, and you were forced to play if you were stupid enough to be out and about on the Day of the Dead. Our two communities had a treaty, signed by the Cráneo Alliance, that cast a spell protecting those that made it to their homes in time for curfew.

But if you weren't inside when the spell cast, you were fair game.

Walking faster, I turned down the alley, bypassing the main road to my home. Papa moved away when Mama died, leaving me their house. He said being here was too hard after her accident. Everything reminded him of her, and he wasn't wrong. Even now, I'd noticed that the leaves were the shade of her favorite cardigan. The brick on the building beside me was the shade of her blush, and the air smelled of cinnamon—like her favorite dessert. And even though my papa and I were close, I stayed behind. I loved my job at the public library. My life was predictable, but it was pleasant. I liked the quiet consistency.

A gust of wind hit me again, this time carrying a teasing whisper, so low that I almost couldn't hear it. Some witches used magic to lure humans out, tempting them to participate in their games. I couldn't help but feel a pricking sense of being followed as I walked, so I increased my strides, desperate to get home.

There was a high pitched laugh behind me, a woman's cackle that made the hairs on the back of my neck stand up. I spun around, looking for the source of the sound but saw nothing. The laughter broke out and echoed off the walls in the alley, making me stumble as I stepped forward.

"Little Human, won't you come out to play?" a light, teasing feminine voice whispered in my ear. I could practically feel the hiss of her breath on my skin, and I shuddered while jogging towards the end of the alley. I glanced down at my watch, gasping when I saw the time.

I only had ten minutes. I could have sworn I had a full hour—at least! Had I been spelled?

"Come on, Little Human. I know all your secrets. You want to see your Mama, don't you? Come here, mija. Let me help you."

Nothing about the voice sounded helpful. In the back of my mind, the part of me that thrived on instinct and could discern between friend or foe, I knew it was just a trick to get me to play the games.

Each witch team needed a human to complete the trials, it was part of the magic. "I don't w-want to," I cried out while spinning around, feeling foolish for speaking to the air. I couldn't see anyone, though my sluggish eyes searched everywhere. Just a little further and I could get home.

"You could see your Mama again," the voice whispered. I felt a gust of wind hit my cheek, directing my attention to the left side of the alley, where a shadowed figure stood. I tried to force my eyes to focus on the wispy shadow, but everything in my mind felt like an echo of reality. There was a delay between what my eyes could see and what my brain could process.

"Camila?" a voice similar to my mother's called out. It didn't feel real, though. It was more like a memory, an echo of the tone my brain constructed then projected across my skull. Somehow I waded through the disorientation to decide that it wasn't her, but the urge to reach out and double check was oh-so-tempting.

"See? Just stay, and I can let you talk to her again," the voice promised. I found myself slowing down and spinning to face the shadow. My brain was screaming at my legs to keep running, to go home

and lock the door, but I couldn't force myself to tear my eyes away. Upon closer inspection, I recognized the long auburn hair and black eyes of my mother. I cocked my head to the side, willing myself to really look at the apparition in front of me. I knew she wasn't real, but I ached for my mother. I missed her hugs, her confidence in me. I missed listening to her make breakfast and humming her favorite songs.

"Just stay, little Camila. I'll help you talk to her again. She misses you terribly," the voice echoed once more as I moved forward. I inched my hands out, wanting to touch the silky material of the ghost's dress and wrap my arms around her for a hug. Would she smell like rose water, my mother's perfume? Could a human also talk to the dead?

Everything felt slow and sluggish as I moved. It was like I couldn't control my muscles. I wondered if the witch cursed me to be suspended in time, leaning to touch the ghost of my mother but never really making that connection. "Mama?" I called out, my voice sounding youthful. I felt like a child again, reaching for the comfort of my mother, wanting to be held close.

I'd hoped that she would respond, reach out to hug

me and tell me one of her cheesy jokes. But instead, it was a man's voice that greeted me.

"Well hello there, Natalia. Playing dirty, I see?" a low voice rumbled, cutting through my fog and confusion. It was different than the tempting whispers of before, clear and precise, it broke through my confusion. "You know it's against the treaty to lure a human out past curfew."

I heard a snapping sound, and the ghost in front of me disappeared, making me cry out. Tears streamed down my cheeks at her sudden disappearance. I wasn't sure why I was so connected to the idea of seeing my mother again, but watching the projection of her dissolve before my eyes made my chest hurt and the grief I'd been feeling this past year swell up within me.

The sounds of heels on concrete made me turn around, and a woman with bleach blond hair strutted down the alley, her arms crossed over her chest as she lifted her hand up and danced her fingers in the air with a dainty wave. "Hello, Luca. Long time, no see," she said while looking over my head. She was wearing an all-black dress with a slit up the thigh.

I turned and flinched when I saw a tall, imposing man standing behind me. His arms were crossed over his chest, honey eyes warm but dark as he stared back at her. They were in a deadly stare off, and I was trapped between them. "You know you can't tease the humans with their memories. That's a cheap move, preying on the poor woman like that," the man named Luca said to her, his eyes squinting as he looked at her with displeasure.

I squeezed my eyes shut, willing myself to be composed. Everything still felt so fuzzy, like my brain was disconnected from the rest of my body. I felt a cold finger on my temple and flinched when I realized it was the man named Luca touching me. For a moment, I tried to shy away, but then a warmth filled my brain, starting at my temple and traveling all the way down to my feet. With it, came a clarity and awareness I didn't have before.

"And a disorientation spell, too? You're disgusting, Natalia," he said to her once more. I shook my head loose of the residual confusion then looked up at him with clear eyes. He was handsome. Sharp features lined his face, and I couldn't help but gape at how...pretty...he looked. He was at least a foot taller than my five foot five inches. His broad chest was covered by a tailored suit that fit *perfectly.* His brown hair looked soft, and it suited his complexion. But more than that, now that my disorientation had worn off, I'd registered that he looked familiar, somehow.

"Thank you," I whispered, suddenly feeling grateful that he'd shown up. I didn't know who this Natalia person was, but I didn't appreciate that she was trying to spell me into being cooperative. I was about to excuse myself but then the community bell tower rang, indicating that curfew had started. I was too late. "Shit!" I called out while looking at my watch.

Natalia sauntered forward, a broad smile on her face as she reached out to me. "Welcome to the Deadly Games, Camila."

Link to The Deadly Games here...